BED OF GRASS

BED OF GRASS

JANET DAILEY

Thorndike Press • Chivers Press
Thorndike, Maine USA   Bath, England

Published in 2000 in the U.S. by arrangement
with Richard Curtis Associates, Inc.

Published in 2000 in the U.K. by arrangement
with the author.

U.S. Hardcover 0-7862-2692-7 (Americana Series Edition)
U.K. Hardcover 0-7540-4273-1 (Chivers Large Print)
U.K. Softcover 0-7540-4274-X (Camden Large Print)

All the characters in this book have no existence outside the
imagination of the author and have no relation whatsoever to
anyone bearing the same name or names. They are not even
distantly inspired by any individual known or unknown to the
author, and all the incidents are pure invention.

The state flower of Maryland is the black eyed Susan.

The text of this Large Print edition is unabridged.
Other aspects of the book may vary from the original edition.

Set in 16 pt. Plantin by Al Chase.

Printed in the United States on permanent paper.

British Library Cataloguing-in-Publication Data available

Library of Congress Cataloging-in-Publication Data

Dailey, Janet.
　　Bed of grass / Janet Dailey.
　　　　p.　　cm.
　　ISBN 0-7862-2692-7 (lg. print : hc : alk. paper)
　　1. Single mothers — Fiction.　2. Maryland — Fiction.
　3. Large type books.　I. Title.
　PS3554.A29 B37 2000
　　813′.54—dc21　　　　　　　　　　　　　　00-034368

BED OF GRASS

CHAPTER ONE

With efficient, precise motions, Valerie Wentworth folded the lingerie and laid it in the suitcase. Tucking a strand of toffee-colored hair behind her ear, she walked back to the open drawer of the dresser for more. There was a determined line to the sensuous curve of her lips and a glint of purpose in her light brown eyes. Her complexion had a hint of shocked pallor under its pale gold tan.

A woman stood in the room watching Valerie pack. Her expression was not altogether approving of what she saw. She was in her forties; her figure had the solid build of middle age and her brown hair was beginning to become frosted with gray. Her mouth was pinched into lines that discouraged smiles.

"I still say you're a fool, Valerie Wentworth, to go tearing off to Maryland like this." The acerbic tongue of the older woman repeated an earlier claim.

"He was my grandfather." Valerie didn't pause in her packing as she walked to the closet and began stripping clothes from the hangers. "He didn't have any other family but me."

"Elias Wentworth didn't want you around when he was alive. What makes you think he'd want you at his funeral?" came the challenging retort.

"He isn't in a position to say what he wants, is he?" A trace of anger was in Valerie's voice, an anger caused by the reference to the estrangement between herself and her grandfather. "And nothing you can say is going to make me change my mind, Clara," she warned.

"That sanctimonious old man turned his back on you seven years ago, at a time when you needed him most," Clara Simons reminded her sternly. "Him and his self-righteous ways," she murmured under her breath with a sniff of contempt. "Despite all the letters you wrote him, you haven't so much as received a Christmas card from him in all this time. He disowned you. Blood ties meant nothing to him. After the way he treated you, I wouldn't think they'd mean anything to you, either."

A tailored suit in a rich dark blue fabric was the closest Valerie came to a mourning outfit; her stringent budget couldn't absorb the cost of a new dress. She was inwardly grateful that changing customs no longer made black mandatory at family funerals.

"Granddad took me in and raised me

after my parents died," she replied to Clara's comment. "I owe him something for that."

"What utter and complete nonsense!" the woman scoffed at her logic. "How can you feel obligated to that heartless, straight-laced coot? Anyone with an ounce of compassion would have stood beside you seven years ago. They might not have approved of what you'd done, but they would have stood with you and not turned a scared girl like you were out in the cold to fend for herself with no money and no place to go."

"You didn't know me when I was a young girl, Clara," stated Valerie. "I was a wild, irresponsible thing, always into trouble. My escapades would have grayed any young man's head. When I was thirteen, I started smoking cigarettes — I used to sneak off to the stables to smoke. Once I almost set the whole place on fire. I heard granddad coming and threw a burning cigarette away, and it landed in some hay. If granddad hadn't spotted it, the stable would have gone up in flames and the horses with it. Granddad had every right to be enraged with me. It scared me when I realized what I'd almost done, but despite the spanking I got, it didn't stop me."

"All youngsters experiment with cigarettes at some time in their lives." Her friend attempted to rationalize Valerie's behavior. "In your case, I wouldn't be surprised if you got into trouble just to gain that insensitive man's attention."

"You don't understand." Valerie sighed and turned to face the woman who had become her friend, her family and her surrogate mother over the last seven years. "It wasn't just the smoking. I drank his drink until he finally had to lock it up in the safe. I'd take one of his thoroughbred horses and go night-riding. I don't know how many times I led a lame horse home after a midnight gallop. They were valuable animals, his livelihood, and I treated them like toys."

"Children can be thoughtless at times," Clara admitted. Her defense of Valerie was not quite as vigorous as before, but she was still steadfast in her loyalty.

"There was more." She was driven to make a full confession, needing to expose her guilt. "I used to steal money from him to hitchhike into Baltimore and go to movies or just buy things. Sometimes I'd be gone all weekend, but I never told him where I'd been. Can you imagine what I put him through?"

"You're being too hard on yourself," was the stubborn reply. "Don't forget that I know what a frightened, love-starved girl you were when I met you."

"Love-starved," Valerie repeated thoughtfully. An ache that still hadn't receded after seven years flickered in her tawny eyes. "Perhaps," she conceded, since it was the easiest explanation. "But I'll never forget the anguish that was in granddad's face the day I told him I was pregnant." In her mind's eye she could still see the look of knife-stabbing pain he had given her. "He was such a moral, upright man that he felt shamed and disgraced by what I'd done. When he demanded to know who the father was and I beligerently refused to tell him, it was the last straw that broke him."

Tears burned her eyes at the memory of that stormy scene. She hid them in a flurry of activity, hurriedly folding the blouse to her blue suit and laying it in the suitcase.

"But to throw you out!" Clara refused to consider her grandfather's actions as justified.

"For a long time I resented him for abandoning me, even hated him," Valerie admitted. "But I was eighteen. Turning me out was probably the best punishment he could have given, because it made me responsible for myself. Now I know the heartache of worrying over a child, and I only regret that I never had the courage to go back and tell granddad how sorry I was for the anguish he suffered because of me."

"And that's your reason for going to his funeral," Clara concluded, crossing her arms in front of her in a stance that suggested disapproval and challenge. "It's an empty gesture, don't you think? And a costly one, too, considering the wages you'll lose."

"Mr. Hanover has given me the time off and I'm entitled to two days of compassionate pay." She tried to dodge the issue as she closed the suitcase and locked it with a decisive snap.

"What about the other three days you'll be taking off?" The pointed reminder pinned Valerie to the spot. "You won't be getting paid for them. And there's the cost of driving all the way to Maryland, too."

"I'll just have to cut back on a few things." She was determined not to consider the financial ramifications of her decision to attend her grandfather's funeral. Somehow she'd weather it.

"Humph!" Clara breathed out the sound. "You're barely making ends meet now."

"That's my problem." Valerie opened a second, smaller suitcase and set it on the bed. "You can't talk me out of going, Clara. You're just wasting your breath."

Walking to the dressing table, she opened a different drawer and took out half a dozen sets of little-boy-sized underpants and socks. When they were in the second suitcase, she began adding pajamas and slacks and shirts.

Clara watched in silence for several seconds, her expression growing more disgruntled. "If you must go, there's no sense in carting Tadd along with you."

"He'll think it's a vacation like all his school friends take in the summer," Valerie reasoned.

"Well, you won't think it's a vacation while you're driving there and back with that bundle of energy bouncing all over the car seats," her friend declared. "What will you do with him when you get there? A six-year-old boy isn't going to understand about funerals . . . or sit through one."

"I don't have much choice." Valerie glanced at the second single bed in the room, a twin to her own, except for the worn, stuffed teddy bear resting against the pillow. She was aware of the validity of Clara's argument.

"I'll look after him," Clara volunteered. There was a grudging quality to her voice, an impatience that she hadn't been able to persuade Valerie not to go.

She glanced at her friend, her strained features softening as she looked at the stern-faced woman. For all her gruffness, Clara had become her rock. She had been the cook in a restaurant Valerie had stumbled into a week after leaving her grandfather's home. She had been frightened, broke and hungry, looking for any kind of job that would put food in her stomach. Clara had taken pity on her, paid for the meal Valerie couldn't afford, persuaded the owner to hire Valerie as a waitress, and taken her to her apartment to live until she could afford a place of her own, which wasn't until after Tadd was born.

"If school weren't over for the summer, Clara, I might accept your offer," Valerie replied, and shook her head in refusal, pale brown curls swinging loosely around her shoulders. "As it is, you've barely recovered from your bout with pneumonia. The doctor insisted you had to rest for a month before going back to work at the restaurant. Looking after Tadd twenty-four hours a day could never be classified as a rest."

"What about Tadd's father? Will you be seeing him when you go back?" A pair of shrewd blue eyes were watching her closely.

A chill of premonition shivered over Valerie's shoulders. Her hands faltered slightly in the act of folding one of Tadd's shirts. The moment of hesitation passed as quickly as it had come and she was once again poised and sure of her decision.

"Probably," Valerie admitted with a show of indifference. "Meadow Farms adjoins granddad's property, so some member of the Prescott family is bound to put in an appearance at the funeral. I don't know whether it will be Judd or not. He runs the farm now so he may not consider the funeral of an insignificant horse breeder to be worthy of his time, neighbor or not. He may deputize someone else to represent the family."

"No woman ever completely forgets the man who takes her virginity, especially if she eventually bears his child. Do you still care about him, Valerie?" came the quiet but piercing question.

A wound that had never completely healed twisted Valerie's heart, squeezing out a bitter hatred that coated her reply. "I wouldn't have married Judd Prescott if he'd begged me — though he's never begged for anything in his life. He takes what he wants without ever giving a damn about anybody's feelings. He's ruthless, hard and arrogant. I

15

was a fool ever to think I was anything more to him than a means to satisfy his lust," she coldly berated herself. "That's why I never told granddad who the father of my baby was. I knew he'd go over to Meadow Farms with a shotgun in his hand, ranting and raving about family honor and scandal, and I would rather have been stoned than see Judd Prescott's derisive amusement at the thought of being forced to marry me."

The suppressed violence in Valerie's denial and rejection of Tadd's father brought a troubled light to Clara's eyes. Her expression was uneasy, but Valerie was too caught up in her own turmoil to notice the gathering silence that met her denunciation. She continued folding and packing her son's clothes into the suitcase.

"Do you know, I believe there's a sensible solution to our problem?" Clara said after the long pause.

"What problem?" Valerie glanced briefly at her friend. There was none as far as she was concerned.

"I'm going crazy sitting around my apartment doing nothing and you're going to have your hands full trying to cope with Tadd on this trip." It was more of a statement than an explanation. "A change of scenery would do me good, so I'll ride along with you to Maryland. Naturally I'll pay my share of the expenses."

"I can't let you do that," Valerie protested. "I'd love to have you come with me — you know that. But you've done so much for me already that I couldn't take any money from you for the trip."

Clara shrugged her wide shoulders, her gaze running over Valerie's shapely, petite figure. "You aren't big enough to stop me." Turning toward the door, she added over her shoulder, "I'll go pack and fix some sandwiches to take along on the trip. I'll be ready in less than an hour."

Before Valerie's lips could form an objection, Clara was gone. A half smile tilted the corners of her mouth when she heard her apartment door closing. Arguing with Clara was useless: once she had made up her mind about something, not even dynamite could budge her.

Valerie didn't like to contemplate what her life might have been like if she hadn't met the other woman. It hadn't simply been food, a place to live or a job that Clara had given her. She had encouraged Valerie to take night courses in secretarial work, to acquire skills that would help her to obtain a better-paying job so she could take care of herself and Tadd.

Many times Valerie had thanked God for guiding her to this woman who was both friend and adviser, supporter and confidante. This gesture of accompanying her made her doubly grateful. Although she hadn't admitted it, she was apprehensive about going back for the funeral. There were a lot of people to be faced, including Judd Prescott.

Walking to the single bed in the corner, Valerie picked up the teddy bear to put in the suitcase. A combination of things made her hold the toy in her arms — the notification a few hours earlier of her grandfather's death, her hurried decision to attend his funeral, her discussion with Clara and the memories attached to her departure from Maryland seven years ago.

Those last were impossible to think about without Judd Prescott becoming entangled with them. Her interest in him had been sparked by a remark she'd overheard her grandfather make condemning the eldest Prescott son for his rakehell reputation. Prior to that Valerie had no interest in the wealthy occupants of Meadow Farms, dismissing them as stiff-necked snobs.

Meadow Farms was a renowned name in racehorse circles, famous for consistently breeding stakes-class thoroughbreds. The farm itself was a showcase, a standard of measure for other horse breeders. Few had ever matched its size or the quality of horses that were bred and raised there.

Her grandfather's low opinion of Judd Prescott had aroused her curiosity. She had ridden onto Meadow Farms land with the express purpose of meeting him. One glimpse of the tall, hard-featured man with ebony hair and devil green eyes had fascinated her. A dangerous excitement seemed to pound through her veins when he looked at her.

In the beginning, Valerie pursued him boldly, almost brazenly, arranging chance encounters that had nothing to do with chance at all. The glint in his eyes seemed to tell her he was aware they weren't, too. It angered her, the way he had silently mocked her initial attempts to flirt with him.

The first few times Judd kissed her, it was with the indulgent air of an adult giving candy to a beguiling child. It didn't take Valerie long to discover that her responses disturbed him and the warm ardency of their kisses became less one-sided.

Her previous experiences with the male sex had been with boys her own age or a year or two older, never with anyone more than ten years her senior. She had kissed many boys, necked with a few, but enough to know that the sensations Judd aroused were not common in an embrace. Also, he was skilled. His mouth knew how to excite her and his hands how to caress her.

What had started out as a lark became something more, and Valerie fell in love with him. Aware that he was a man with experience, she realized that her kisses wouldn't hold his interest for long, and her fear of losing him outweighed her fear of the unknown.

One afternoon Valerie noticed him riding alone through a wooded pasture adjoining her grandfather's land. Saddling a horse, she swallowed her nervousness and her pride and rode out to meet him. They rode only a short distance together before pausing to dismount under the shade of a tree. An embrace followed naturally. When Valerie demanded that he make love to her, Judd's hesitation was brief, his affirmative response given in a burning kiss.

Afterward he was oddly uncommunicative, an expressionless glitter in his green eyes whenever they were directed at her. Valerie suspected it was because he was the first to know her. Secretly she wanted him to be disturbed by the fact, to feel a little obligated, perhaps even guilty. Because she loved him so intensely, she had subconsciously attempted to blackmail him emotionally, making him the seducer and herself the innocent victim. When they parted he had said nothing, but Valerie was unconcerned.

Days went by without her seeing him before she finally realized that Judd was avoiding her. Hurt grew into indignation and finally a smoldering anger. Her injured pride demanded revenge. She began haunting the edges of the Meadow Farms stable yard, hoping to catch Judd alone.

At the sight of the luxury sports car that Judd usually drove coming slowly up the paddocked driveway to the stable, Valerie set her fleet-footed horse on a route that would intersect the car's path before it reached its destination. Jumping her mount over a paddock fence, she halted it in the middle of the road to block the way. The car's brakes were applied sharply to bring it to a skidding stop before hitting her.

Judd came storming out of the driver's side of the car, his features stone-cold with rage. "What the hell were you trying to do? Get yourself killed?" His icy gaze flicked to the lathered horse, dancing nervously under her tight rein. "And if you don't give a damn about yourself, you have no business

21

abusing blooded animals that way. His mouth will be raw if you don't quit sawing on those reins."

"Don't tell me how to ride a horse! And what do you care what happens to me anyway!" Valerie had flamed. "At least I know what kind of a low, contemptible man you are! You take a girl's virginity, then drop her cold!!"

"I didn't want it." Judd drew out the denial through clenched teeth. "Considering the reputation you have, I thought you'd lost it years ago."

Valerie went white with rage at his insulting remark. She jabbed her heels into the sides of her hunter, sending it lunging toward the tall, insolent man. He stepped to the side and she began striking at him with her riding crop. Catching hold of the end, Judd pulled her from the saddle. Her horse then bolted for home pastures.

After he had twisted the riding quirt out of her grip, he crushed her twisting, kicking body against him. "You little she-cat, I should use this on you!" His savagely muttered threat made Valerie struggle all the more wildly, cursing and swearing at him, calling him every name she could think of. He laughed cruelly. "Your language would put a stablehand to shame!"

An animallike scream of frustration sounded in her throat, but immediately his mouth bruised her lips to punish them into silence. The dominating quality of his kiss subdued the rest of her until the only twisting Valerie did was to get closer to his leanly muscled frame.

When his mouth ended its possession of hers, she whispered, "Make love to me again, Judd."

"You damned little temptress." But his voice was husky with passion, the smoldering light in his green eyes fanning her trembling desire.

Valerie received the answer she wanted when he swept her off her feet into his arms and carried her to a secluded bed of grass that was to become their meeting place during the following months.

What Valerie lacked in experience, she made up for in willingness. Under the guidance of a master in the art of love, she learned rapidly. Over the course of time it became evident to her that Judd desired her as much as she desired him. Secure in this knowledge, it never bothered her that he didn't take her out anywhere. Besides, there was her grandfather's wrath to be considered if he should find out about the two of them.

Even when she first suspected she was pregnant, she wasn't worried. Nor later, when she hitched a ride to Baltimore to a medical clinic for confirmation of her condition, was she apprehensive. She was certain Judd would be as pleased as she was about the news and would be moved to propose.

She was saddling a horse to ride over to Meadow Farms when her grandfather walked up. "Where you going?" he demanded.

Valerie responded with a half-truth, patting the sleek neck of the bay horse. "I thought I'd take Sandal out for a canter, maybe over toward Meadow Farms." Just in case he would see her heading in that direction.

"The place will probably be bustling with activity, what with the party and all," he commented in a disapproving way.

"What party?" It had been the first Valerie had heard about one.

"The Prescotts are having one of their lavish society affairs tonight." His eyes narrowed on her in accusing speculation. "And don't you be getting any ideas about crashing it. No granddaughter of mine is going to get involved with such carrying-on."

"Yes, granddad." Despite the feigned meekness of her tone, a vision had already begun to form of Judd possessively holding her hand while he introduced her to friends and family at the party.

Wrapped in her romantic imaginings, Valerie rode off to the secluded place in the wooded pasture where they always met, but Judd wasn't there. Even though the meeting hadn't been prearranged, she was positive he would appear. Within minutes after she had dismounted, he rode into the clearing.

There were so many things she wanted to tell him in that instant: how ruggedly handsome he was, how much she loved him, about the baby — their baby — and how ecstatically happy she was. But something made her keep all that inside. She even turned away when he dismounted and plucked a green leaf from a low-hanging branch.

"It's a beautiful day, isn't it?" she observed instead.

"Beautiful," came his husky agreement from directly behind her.

When his hands circled her waist to cup her breasts and draw her shoulders against his chest, Valerie breathed in sharply and exhaled in a sigh of pure pleasure. Her head lolled backward against his chest while his mouth moved against the windblown waves of her caramel hair.

"How do you always know when I come here?" she murmured, the wonder of it something she had never questioned before.

"A fire starts burning inside of me, here." His hand slid low on her stomach to indicate the location, his mouth moving against her hair as he spoke.

Valerie turned in his arms, in answer to the flames he had started within her. Hungrily he began devouring her lips and she felt herself begin to surrender to his appetite. But she wanted to talk. Finally she dragged her lips from the domination of his, letting his mouth wander over her cheek and ear and nibble sensuously at her throat.

"I thought you wouldn't come today," she said weakly.

"Why?" Judd sounded amused.

"Because of the party." Her limbs were turning to water.

"That isn't until tonight." He dismissed its importance, but made no suggestion that she should attend.

Valerie understood why no invitation had been given to her grandfather. He was not in the Prescotts' social or financial sphere. Besides, he was morally opposed to drinking and dancing. He would have considered it an offense to be invited, not a courtesy.

"I've never been to a party like that before." Valerie tried not to be too open about seeking an invitation. "It must be grand. I suppose the women will be wearing diamonds and beautiful gowns."

"In all their clothes, none of them will look lovelier than you do without any." Even as he spoke, his hands were unbuttoning her blouse.

Valerie attempted to gently forestall his efforts. "Why didn't you invite me?" Her question was light, not betraying how much she wanted to know.

"You wouldn't like it." His mouth worked its way to the hollow of her throat, tipping her head back to allow greater access.

"How do you know?" She strained slightly against his hold.

Judd lifted his head, ebony hair gleaming in the sunlight. Impatience was written behind his lazy regard. A firmness strengthened the line of his mouth.

"Because it isn't your kind of party," he replied in a tone that said the discussion was at an end.

At that moment fear began to gnaw at Valerie's confidence. Proud defiance was present in the way she returned his look.

"Maybe you aren't inviting me because you've made arrangements to take somebody else," she challenged.

"It isn't any of your business." A cold smile touched his mouth as it began to descend toward hers.

Hurt by his attitude as much as his words, Valerie tried to draw out of his arms. Her blouse gaped open in the front and his gaze roamed downward to observe the creamy globes of her breasts nearly spilling free of her lacy bra. His hand moved to help them, but she managed to stop it.

"Please, I want to talk, Judd," she insisted.

"Why waste energy with words when it can be put to more pleasurable use?" he argued, and pressed her hips against his so she could feel his urgent need for her.

With a sickening rush of despair, she realized that they seldom talked when they met. They made love, rested and went their separate ways. Their past communications had always been physical, never verbal. Valerie suddenly saw what a fool she had been to think otherwise.

"Let me go!" She pushed angrily at his chest, the yellow lights in her pale brown eyes flashing warning signals of temper.

"What's this little display of outrage

about?" Judd eyed her with cynical amusement, holding her but no longer forcing her close to him. "After as many times as we've made love together, it's a little late to be playing hard to get."

Her temper flared, adrenalin surging through her muscles to give them strength, and she broke out of his encircling arms.

"That's all I mean to you, isn't it?" she accused. "I'm just someone to roll around on the grass with, someone to satisfy your lusts. To you, I'm nothing but a cheap little tramp. I'm not good enough for you to be seen in public with!"

"You'd better sheathe your claws, tigress. You're the one who invited me into your bed of grass," Judd reminded her with deadly calm.

A couple of long jerky strides carried Valerie to the place where her horse was tethered. She gathered up the reins and mounted before turning to face him.

"I hope you go to hell, Judd Prescott." Her voice had begun to tremble. "And I hope it's a long, hot trip!"

Putting her heels to her mount, she turned and galloped the horse toward her grandfather's farm. Tears drenched her cheeks with hot, salty moisture. All her rosy dreams were shattered that day when she realized Judd had never felt more than desire for her.

An hour later she informed her grand-father that she was pregnant, immune to his wrath when she refused to tell him it was Judd who had fathered the life she carried. It was almost a relief when he ordered her out of the house. She put as much distance between herself and Maryland as possible.

That was how she had ended up here in Cincinnati, Ohio, living in the same apartment complex as Clara, with an illegitimate six-year-old son, and a job as secretary to an industrial plant executive.

Her cheeks felt hot and wet. She lifted the hand that had been clutching the teddy bear and touched her fingers to her face. They came away wet with tears. The wound inside her was as raw and fresh as it had been seven years ago. She scrubbed her cheeks dry with the back of her hands and blinked her eyes to ease the stinging sensation.

"Mom!"

A three-foot-tall whirlwind came racing into the bedroom. It stopped its motion long enough for her to gaze into a pair of hazel eyes predominantly shaded with olive green. Hair a darker shade of brown than her own fell across his forehead, crowding into his eyes.

"Clara said I was to come into the house. You said I could play outside until you called me," he declared in a breathless rush, already edging toward the door again. "Can I go back out? It's my turn after Tommy's to ride Mike's Big Wheels. What are you doing with Toby?" He saw the teddy bear in her arms.

"I was just packing him in your suitcase," she explained. "We're going on a trip, remember?"

Tadd momentarily forgot his turn on the Big Wheels. "Where's Maryland?"

"It's a long way from here. We'll have to drive all day." Valerie laid the teddy bear on top of his suitcase. "We'll be ready to go soon, so you'd better wash your face and hands and change into those clean clothes." She pointed to the colored T-shirt and jeans lying on the bed.

Tadd made a face when she told him he had to wash. "Why are we going to Maryland?"

"Because your great-grandfather died and I want to go to his funeral," she answered patiently.

"Why?"

Valerie concealed a sigh. She was never certain whether his questions were asked out of genuine interest or as an excuse to postpone something he didn't want to do.

"When I was your age, I didn't have a mommy, so your great-grandfather took care of me. I cared about him the way you care about me. That's why I want to go to his funeral."

"Did I know him?" Tadd tilted his head to one side, his expression showing only innocent curiosity.

"No." Valerie shook her head.

Her teeth nibbled at the inside of her lower lip. She had written to her grandfather about Tadd's birth, but had never received any form of acknowledgement. None of the letters she had regularly sent had ever been answered.

"Do I have a grandfather?" He altered the subject slightly.

Valerie hesitated. The only relatives Tadd had that were still living were on the Prescott side. But for the time being it was better if he didn't know about them. The time would come soon enough for him to learn about his heritage.

"No." Not legally, she defended her lie.

"If you died, there wouldn't be anybody to take care of me, would there? I'd be an orphan," he stated with a round-eyed look.

"Clara would look after you," Valerie reassured him, bending to kiss his forehead before he could dodge away. "Go and wash." She administered a playful spank to his backside as he scampered toward the bathroom. "You'd better hurry, too," she called the warning after him. "Clara's coming with us and you know how upset she gets if people aren't ready on time."

CHAPTER TWO

Valerie had done most of the driving, with Clara spelling her for an hour every so often to give her a rest. They had traveled well into the night before stopping at an inexpensive motel along the highway for a few hours' sleep. The morning sun was in their faces, its light shining on the countryside of Maryland.

"How long before we get there, mom?" Tadd piped the question from the back seat and leaned over the middle armrest to hear her answer.

"To save the wear and tear on your vocal cords, Tadd, we should have tape-recorded that question when we started out." Behind the searing dryness of Clara's voice, there was a hint of amused tolerance. "You must have asked it a thousand times."

"How long, mom?" he repeated.

"Not long. We'll be seeing the lane to the farm any minute now." Valerie discovered her hands were gripping the steering wheel until her knuckles were white.

Seven years had brought some changes to the area where she had once lived, but they had just driven past the entrance gates to

Meadow Farms. Charcoal black fences marked off its paddocks. Just over that far hill near that stand of trees was the place where she used to meet Judd. It was one place she would have preferred to forget.

"That's a fancy-looking place," Clara observed, but her eyes were on her companion when Valerie shot her a startled look.

"Yes," she agreed nervously. "It's the Prescott place." She knew she was confirming what Clara had already guessed.

"Look at all the horses!" Tadd breathed, pressing his face against a side window. "Did they ever let you ride them when you were a kid, mom?"

"I didn't ride any of those, but your grandfather owned horses. He raised them," Valerie explained, shifting the subject away from the breeding farm they were passing. "I used to ride his."

"You can ride?" There was a squeak of disbelief in his voice. "Gee, I wish I had a horse."

"Where would you keep it?" Clara wanted to know. "It's too big for the apartment. Besides, you're not allowed to have pets."

"When I get big, I'm going to move out of there and get me a horse," Tadd stated, his tone bordering on a challenge.

"When you get big, you'll want a car," Clara retorted.

"No, I won't." After the confinement of the car for almost twelve hours, Tadd was beginning to get irritable. Usually he enjoyed arguing with Clara, but he was starting to sound mutinous.

"Here's granddad's place." Valerie distracted his attention as she turned the car onto a narrow dirt lane.

A sign hung from a post on the left-hand side. The paint had faded, but enough of the letters were still distinguishable to make out the name Worth Farms, a shortened appellation of Wentworth. Board fences flanked the lane. Once they had been painted white, but the sun had blistered the paint away, leaving the wood grayed and weathered. Half a dozen mares with foals could be seen grazing in the green carpet of grass in the pasture.

"Look, Tadd." Valerie pointed to the opposite side of the car from where he was sitting. "There are horses here, too."

But not for long, she thought to herself. With her grandfather gone, they would be sold off, and the farm, too. It was difficult to accept that the place she had always regarded as home would soon belong to someone else. It was a sorrow, a resigned regret. Valerie had no hard feelings against her grandfather for disinheriting her; she had given him ample cause as a teenager.

"Can we stop and see the horses, mom?" Tadd bounced anxiously in the back seat, not satisfied with the slowed pace of the car that gave him a long time to watch the sleek, glistening animals.

"Later," Valerie qualified her refusal.

"Promise?" he demanded.

"I promise," she agreed, and let her gaze slide to Clara, whose shrewd eyes were inspecting the property. "The house and barns are just ahead." The roofs and part of the structures were in view.

"Are you sure there'll be somebody there?" Clara questioned with dry skepticism.

"Mickey Flanners will be there. I know he'll let us stay long enough to wash and clean up. We can find out from him the details about the funeral arrangements and all," she explained, and smiled briefly. "You'll like Mickey," she told her friend. "He's an ex-jockey. He's worked for granddad for years, taking care of the horses and doing odd jobs around the place. He's probably looking after things now until all the legal matters are settled and the farm . . . is sold." Again she felt the twinge of regret that this was no longer her home, not when her grandfather was alive nor now. She covered the pause with a quick, "Mickey is a lovable character."

"Which means he's short and fat, I suppose." The cutting edge of Clara's statement was blunted by her droll brand of humor.

"Short and pudgy," Valerie corrected with a twinkling look.

As they entered the yard of the horse farm, the barns and stables were the first to catch her eye. Although they were in need of a coat of paint, they were in good repair. Valerie hadn't expected differently. Her grandfather had never allowed anything to become run-down. The two-story house was in the same shape, needing paint but well kept. The lawn was overgrown with weeds in dire need of mowing.

Her sweeping inspection of the premises ended as her gaze was caught by a luxury-model car parked in front of the house. A film of dust coated the sides, picked up from dirt roads. A tingling sensation danced over her nerve ends. Her mouth felt dry and she swallowed convulsively.

"Did you really used to live here, mom?" Tadd's eager voice seemed to come from a great distance.

"Yes." Her answer was absent.

"I wish I did," was his wistful response.

Automatically Valerie parked beside the other car. It could belong to any number of people, she told herself, a lawyer, a banker, someone from the funeral home, just anyone. But somehow she knew better.

The car's engine had barely stopped turning before Tadd was opening the back door and scrambling out. Valerie followed his lead, but in a somewhat dazed fashion. A small hand grabbed hold of hers and tugged to pull her away from the house.

"Let's go see the horses, mom," Tadd demanded. "You promised we would."

"Later." But she was hardly conscious of answering him. An invisible magnet was pulling her toward the house, its compelling force stronger than the pleadings of her son.

"I want to go now!" His angry declaration fell on deaf ears.

The screen door onto the front porch opened and a man stepped onto the painted board floor. The top buttons of his white shirt were unfastened, exposing the bronze skin of his hair-roughened chest. Long sleeves had been rolled back, revealing the corded muscles of his forearms. The white of his shirt tapered to male hips, dark trousers stretching the length of his supple, muscled legs.

But it was the unblinking stare of green eyes that held Valerie in their thrall. Fine lines fanned out from the corners of them. Harsh grooves were etched on either side of his mouth, carved into sun-browned skin stretched leanly from cheekbone to jawline. His jet black hair was in casual disorder that was somehow sensuous.

Her heart had stopped beating at the sight of Judd, only to start up again at racing speed to send the blood pounding hotly through her veins. The seven years melted away until they were no longer ago than yesterday. Untold pleasures were no farther away than the short distance that separated them. That chiseled mouth had only to take possession of hers to transport her to the world of secret delights.

The compulsion was strong to take the last few steps to reach that hard male body. Valerie would have succumbed to it if the small hand holding hers hadn't tugged her arm to demand her attention. Reluctantly she dragged her gaze from Judd and glanced down to the small boy at her side. Only a few seconds had passed instead of years.

"Who's that man?" Tadd frowned, eyeing Judd with a look that was both puzzled and wary.

Valerie couldn't help wondering what

would happen if she told him Judd was his father. But of course she couldn't, and didn't. Tadd's question had succeeded in bringing her to her senses. Valerie realized the painful truth that the aching rawness of her desire for Judd hadn't diminished over the years of separation, but she was equally determined not to become enslaved by that love as she had been seven years ago.

Her gaze swung back to Judd, her amber-flecked eyes masked. "It's a neighbor, Judd Prescott." Her voice sounded remarkably calm.

A muttered sigh came from Clara, issued low for Valerie's ears alone. "I didn't think it was your lovable Mickey." Her comment implied that she had guessed Judd's identity the minute he stepped out of the house.

Valerie didn't have time to acknowledge her friend's remark, for Judd was walking down the porch steps to greet her. He extended a hand toward her.

"Welcome home, Valerie." His low-pitched voice carried little other expression than courtesy. "I'm sorry your return is under these circumstances."

His words of sympathy were just that — words. They carried no sincerity. A bitter surge of resentment made her want to hurl them back in his face. One look at his hard features cast in bronze told her he was incapable of feelings, except the baser kind.

Valerie swallowed the impulse and murmured a stiff, "I'm sorry, too."

Unconsciously she placed her hand in his. When she felt the strong grip of his fingers closing over her own, she was struck by the irony of the situation. She was politely and impersonally shaking hands with a man who knew her more intimately than anyone ever had, a man who was the father of her child. There wasn't any part of her that the hand she held hadn't explored many times and with devastating thoroughness. She felt the beginnings of a trembling desire and withdrew her hand from his before she betrayed it.

"I'm Tadd." Her son demanded his share of the attention.

Her hand drifted to his small shoulder. "This is my son," she told Judd, and watched his reaction.

He didn't seem surprised by her announcement, nor was there any suspicion in his expression that he was looking into the face of his child. Valerie supposed that she saw the faint resemblance between the two because she knew and was looking for it.

"Hello, Tadd." Judd bent slightly at the waist to shake hands with the boy. It was a gesture minus the warmth of affection or friendliness, prompted only by courtesy.

At first Tadd seemed slightly overwhelmed by the action. Then a smile of importance widened his mouth. "Hello," he replied.

Valerie realized it was the first time an adult had ever shaken hands with him; usually they rumpled his hair and tweaked his chin. No wonder he was looking so proud and important! She was almost angry with Judd for being the one to treat Tadd as something other than a pet, because she knew he meant nothing by it. She stifled the rush of antagonism and turned to introduce him to Clara.

"Clara, this is Judd Prescott. He owns the land that adjoins my grandfather's." The explanation was unnecessary, but Valerie made it to show Judd that she hadn't found him important enough to discuss with her friend prior to their arrival. "This is my friend Mrs. Clara Simons."

"I'm pleased to meet you, Mrs. Simons." Judd issued the polite phrase and shook Clara's hand.

"Likewise, I'm sure." Clara returned the polite phrasing, while the two of them eyed each other like a pair of opponents taking the measure of one another's strengths and weaknesses. Tension seemed to crackle in the air.

"I didn't expect to see you here when we arrived, Judd." Valerie's brittle comment was a challenge to explain his presence on the farm. "I thought we'd find Mickey instead."

"Did you?" The gleam in his eyes seemed to taunt her statement, but Judd went on smoothly without waiting for a reply. "Mick is here. I just stopped by to check on things and see if there was any way I could be of assistance."

"A neighborly call, hmm?" Clara's sharp voice questioned his motive with mockery.

But he remained unscathed by the jibe, his cat green gaze swinging to the stoutly built woman unperturbed. "Something like that," he agreed. Turning to one side, he called toward the house, "Mick? Valerie has arrived."

"You don't say!" came the muffled exclamation in a lilting tenor voice that Valerie remembered well, and seconds later a short squat figure came bustling out of the house. Mickey looked older and wasn't as agile as she remembered. The wispy crop of hair on his head still reminded her of straw, but it was thinner. "As I live and breathe, it's Valerie!"

"Hello, Mickey." She smiled, unaware of the warmth and affection her expression held or the way Judd's eyes narrowed into green slits at the unconsciously alluring transformation.

With slightly bowed legs, Mickey Flanners was built so close to the ground that he appeared to tumble down the steps to greet her. A head shorter than she was, he clasped one of her hands in the powerful grip of both of his. She realized that his hands still had the strength to control the most fractious of horses.

"I got word yesterday afternoon that you was coming for the funeral, but I didn't know how soon you'd get here." His knowledge was of horses, not subjects like grammar, but his brand of reckless Irish charm made it easy to overlook.

"We drove practically straight through," Valerie explained. "We stopped here before going into town to rest and find out the details about the funeral arrangements. I thought you would know about them."

"Of course I do. You —" Mickey began, only to be interrupted by Tadd.

"You aren't even as tall as my mom. When are you going to grow up?" he wanted to know.

"Mind your tongue, Tadd!" It was Clara

who snapped out the reproval, but Valerie just smiled and Mickey laughed, never having been sensitive about his size, and Judd's green eyes simply observed.

"To tell you the truth, me lad —" Mick adopted a poor imitation of an Irish brogue and winked at Valerie "— I don't intend to ever grow up," he confided to Tadd in a loud whisper. "Wouldn't you like to stay little like me all your life?"

Without hesitation, Tadd made a negative shake of his head. "No, I want to grow tall like him." He pointed at Judd.

Valerie caught her breath at the amused twitch of Judd's mouth. But he didn't know it was his son who wanted to grow up like him. At the rate Tadd was growing out of his clothes, she guessed he probably would top the six-foot mark like Judd.

"Well, if that's the way you feel about it, there's nothing I can do." Mickey looked properly crestfallen, but laughter danced in the eyes as he turned toward Valerie. "Where's your luggage? I'll carry it in the house for you."

"We were planning to stay at a motel in town." Valerie's instinctive response was a protest.

"A motel?" Mickey stepped back. "Eli would have my hide if I let you and the boy stay at a motel! I mean — if he was alive," he corrected with a sobering look. "You're the only family he had. There's no sense in sleeping in a strange place when your old bedroom is empty."

"Our luggage is in the trunk of the car and the keys are in the ignition." Clara offered this information while Valerie was still absorbing Mickey's reply.

He had made it sound as if her grandfather would have wanted her back. And he had known about Tadd, and obviously hadn't kept it a secret or Mickey would not have taken his presence for granted. For that reason alone Valerie wasn't going to argue about staying, discounting the fact that she could ill afford the cost of the motel room.

Mickey's ebullient spirits could never be battened down for long. They surfaced again as he obtained the key from the ignition and walked to the rear of the car to unlock the trunk. He began unloading the suitcases, chattering continuously.

"When you left here, Valerie, old Eli seemed to lose heart. He didn't quit or anything like that — he'd never give up his horses — but he just didn't seem to have the enthusiasm anymore." Mickey paused to glance around the place. "For the last three

47

years he'd been talking about painting everything, but he never got around to it. The truth is I don't think he had the money to hire it done and neither one of us was spry enough to paint it ourselves. And you know your grandfather: if he couldn't pay cash for what he wanted, he did without." He set the last suitcase on the ground. "Is this all of them?"

"Yes," Valerie nodded.

He glanced down at them. "Guess I'll have to make two trips."

"I'll help you carry them inside, Mick," Judd volunteered, as the ex-jockey had expected him to do. Judd was aware of Mickey's tactics, but appeared tolerant.

"Thanks, Judd." Mickey picked out the heaviest suitcases and handed them to him.

That was when Valerie noticed that Tadd had tagged along after Judd. He tipped his dark head way back to look up at him, a determinedly adult look on his childish face.

"I can carry one," he insisted.

"Do you think so?" Judd's glance was indulgent and tolerant, but indifferent. He nodded toward Valerie's makeup case. "That one looks about your size. Can you handle it?"

"Sure." Tadd picked it up with both hands. It bounced against his knees as he walked behind Judd toward the house.

"I'll tell you one thing, Valerie," Mickey was saying as he led the way up the porch steps and into the house. "Your granddad sure perked up when he found out he had a great-grandchild. Proud as a peacock, he was, passing out cigars to anybody that came within hailing distance."

A lump entered Valerie's throat. Her grandfather had been proud; he hadn't been ashamed when he learned of Tadd's birth. Why hadn't he let her know? She would have brought Tadd for him to see. Hadn't he realized that she had expected her reception to be a door slamming in her face?

"Ain't got no coffee made," Mick added. "But I guess you could make a pot while we take the luggage to your rooms. Ain't nothing been changed since you left, so the fixings are where they always were. You know what old Eli said: 'a place for everything and everything in its place,'" he quoted the old adage that her grandfather had recited many times.

"A cup of coffee is just what I need," Clara stated briskly. "You go and fix some, Valerie, while I see to our luggage and hang our clothes up before they're permanently wrinkled."

Valerie was left downstairs to make her

49

way to the kitchen while the rest of them climbed the steps to the second-floor bedrooms. She hadn't realized how tense she had been in Judd's presence until she was away from him. Her severely controlled nerves seemed to almost shudder in relief when she stood alone in the simple farm kitchen. She had wanted that fiery attraction between them to be dead, but it wasn't — not for her.

She heard footsteps approaching the kitchen, more than one set, and began filling the coffeepot with water. She turned off the taps as Judd entered the kitchen, followed closely by Tadd and Mickey.

"I saw the bedroom where you slept as a little kid, mom," Tadd announced, bouncing over to the counter and standing on tiptoe to see what she was doing. "Mickey showed it to me. He said it was the same bed you used to sleep in. Can I sleep in it, mom?"

"Yes, you may sleep in my bed if you want to," she agreed, and turned to open the cupboard on her left.

Her gaze encountered Judd's. She had the disturbing sensation that she had just given permission to him instead of her son. The canister of coffee was where it had always been kept. Her shaking hands lifted it down to the counter top as she turned to avoid the glitter of his eyes.

"When can we go see the horses?" Tadd reverted to his previous theme.

"Later on. I told you that before," Valerie replied with a hint of impatience creeping through.

"But it is later," he reasoned. "And you promised."

"Tadd, I'm making coffee." She shot him a warning look not to pursue the issue and his lower lip jutted out in a pout.

"So it's horses you're wanting to see, is it, lad?" Mickey's lilting voice brought the light of hope back into Tadd's hazel green eyes.

"Yes, would you take me?" he asked unashamedly.

"First I have to find out how bad you want to see them," Mick cautioned, and walked over to open a cupboard drawer. "You can either have a piece of candy —" he held up a chocolate bar "— or you can come with me to see the horses. Which will it be?"

Except to glance at the candy, Tadd didn't hesitate. "The horses."

Mickey tossed him the chocolate bar. "Spoken like a true horseman! Your great-granddaddy would have been proud to hear you say that."

Tadd stared at the candy. "Aren't you going to take me to see the horses?"

"Of course, lad." Mickey reassured him with a wink. "But you'll be needin' some energy for the walk, won't you?"

"You mean I can have both?" Tadd wanted to be sure before he tore off the paper wrapping around the bar.

"Isn't that what I just said?" Mick teased, and moved toward the back door. "Come along, lad. And don't you be worrying about him, Valerie. I'll watch over him the same as I watched over you."

Valerie had enjoyed watching Mickey work his Irish charm on her son. It wasn't until the door shut that she realized she had been left alone in the kitchen with Judd. What was keeping Clara, she wondered desperately, but was determined not to lose her composure.

"Mickey has always had a way with children," she said into the silence, not risking a glance at Judd as she spooned the coffee grounds into the percolator basket.

"That's because there's a little bit of truth in the fact that he's never grown up." Judd had moved closer. Valerie was fully aware of his disconcerting gaze watching her. He leaned a hip against the counter a few feet from where she worked and entered her line of vision. "I knew you were coming," he said with studied quietness.

She glanced up, the implication of his words jolting through her. Judd had meant that he had known she was coming the same way he had always known when she would be at their meeting place, and she didn't want to know that.

Deliberately she pretended she was unaware of a hidden meaning in his comment. "Word gets around fast, doesn't it? I did tell the hospital when they called that I'd be coming as soon as I could. I suppose everyone in the area knows it by now." She put the lid on the coffeepot and plugged the cord into a socket. Out the kitchen window she could see Tadd skipping alongside Mickey on their way to the barns. "I suppose you're finally married and have a family of your own now." She turned away, trying not to picture Judd in the arms of some beautiful debutante.

"No, to both of those." An aloofness had entered his chiseled features when she glanced at him. "You've matured into a beautiful woman, Valerie." It was a statement, flatly issued, yet with the power to stir her senses as only Judd could.

"Thank you." She tried to accept his words as merely a compliment, but she didn't know how successful she had been.

"I'm sorry your husband wasn't able to accompany you. I would have liked to meet him," he said.

"My husband? Who told you I was married?" Except for startled surprise, there was little expression in her face.

"Your grandfather, of course." He tilted his head to one side, black hair gleaming in a shaft of sunlight.

Valerie realized that she should have guessed her grandfather would come up with a story like that in order to claim his great-grandson without feeling shame.

"That was rather a foolish question for me to ask, wasn't it?" she commented dryly.

Judd didn't make any comment to that. "I suppose he wasn't able to get time off from his job."

Valerie was toying with the idea of revealing her grandfather's lie and correcting Judd's impression that she wasn't married. When she had decided, shortly after Tadd was born, to keep him rather than give him up for adoption, she had accepted the fact that she would have to live with the illegitimacy of his birth, and refused to hide behind a phony wedding ring.

Before she could tell Judd that she had no husband and never did, Clara walked into the kitchen. She glanced from Valerie to Judd and back to Valerie.

"Where's Tadd?" she asked.

"Mickey took him out to see the horses," Valerie explained.

"Is the coffee done?" Clara sat down in one of the kitchen chairs, making it clear that she wasn't budging. "Will you be staying for coffee, Mr. Prescott?" Behind the question was a challenge to explain the reason he was still here.

"No, I don't believe so." Amusement glinted in his green eyes at the belligerently protective attitude of the older woman. His attention returned to Valerie. "The funeral home will be open from six until eight this evening so your grandfather's friends can come to pay their respects. You're welcome to ride in with me if you wish."

"It's kind of you to offer, but we'll find our own way." Valerie refused in the politest of tones.

He inclined his head in silent acceptance of her decision. Bidding them both an impersonal goodbye, Judd left. Neither woman spoke until they heard the roar of a powerful engine starting up at the front of the house.

"Well?" Clara prompted.

"Well, what?" Valerie was deliberately obtuse.

"Well, what did he have to say?" Clara demanded in gruffly autocratic tones.

"Nothing, really, if you mean any reference to our former . . . relationship." Valerie removed two cups from the cabinet above the stove.

"Did he say anything to you about Tadd?"

"No. Judd thinks I'm married. It's a story granddad cooked up."

"Did you tell him differently?" Clara wanted to know, an eyebrow lifting.

"I started to when you walked in," admitted Valerie, and shrugged. "I suppose it's just as well I didn't. Whether I'm supposedly married or single, it doesn't change anything."

"Are you going to tell him that Tadd is his son?"

"If he asks me, I will. What difference does it make?" Valerie said diffidently. "He has no legal right to Tadd — I've seen to that. There isn't anything he could do if he wanted to, which I doubt."

"But he still gets to you, doesn't he?" Clara's voice was understanding and vaguely sad.

"Yes," Valerie sighed. "After all this time, I'm still not immune to him. He's a rotten, insensitive brute, but he would only have to hold me to make me forget that."

"Don't let him hurt you again, honey." It was almost a plea.

Shaking the honey-dark mane of her hair, Valerie curved her mouth into a weak smile. "I'm not going to give him the chance!"

CHAPTER THREE

At a quarter past six that evening Valerie slowed the car to park it in front of the funeral home of the small Maryland community. A few cars were already in the lot.

"Is this where we're going?" Tadd was draped half in the front seat and half in the back.

"Yes." Valerie glanced at him briefly. His little bow tie was already askew and his shirt was coming loose from the waistband of his trousers. "Clara, would you mind tucking his shirt in and straightening his tie?"

"Hold still!" Clara ordered when the boy tried to squirm away. "I don't know if it's a good idea to bring him along."

"He's old enough to understand what's going on," Valerie replied calmly.

"Are we going to a funeral?" Tadd asked.

"No, granddad's funeral is tomorrow," she answered patiently.

"What's a funeral?" At his question, Clara sniffed, a sound that indicated Valerie was wrong to believe Tadd knew what was going on.

"A funeral is when a person dies and all

his friends and family come to say goodbye to him. Do you remember when your turtle died? We put him in a box, buried him in the ground and asked God to take care of him for you because you couldn't."

"Is that a funeral?" Tadd was plainly fascinated by the discovery.

"Yes, that's a funeral." Valerie parked the car next to the curb. "Let's go inside. Remember, Tadd, you promised me you'd be good."

"I will." He tossed off the agreement as he eagerly climbed out of the car.

The hushed atmosphere inside temporarily impressed Tadd. He stood quietly at her side, holding her hand while Valerie spoke to the funeral director. Several of her grandfather's friends had already arrived. Some Valerie remembered; others she didn't.

Tadd had little interest in the condolences the strangers offered. He was too busy looking around him in awed silence. He mutely nodded at Judd when the older man arrived and came over to speak to him and Valerie.

Valerie realized she was clenching her jaw in tension and tried to relax. "Granddad was acquainted with just about everybody in the area, wasn't he?" she remarked.

"Everyone didn't agree with his strict code, but they respected him," Judd stated. "Have you had a chance to go up front?"

Valerie glanced towards the satin-lined casket. "No. Each time I started, someone stopped to offer their sympathies."

"Come on." His arm curved impersonally behind her to rest his hand on the small of her back.

The heat of his touch seemed to send a fire racing up her spine. She was powerless to resist his guidance. Her fingers curled tightly around Tadd's small hand, bringing him along with her.

At the open casket Judd stopped, and Valerie looked on her grandfather's image for the first time in seven years. He looked old and tired lying there, in need of the rest he had obtained. She wanted to tell him how much she loved him and how sorry she was for hurting him, but she had said both many times in the letters she had written him, so she guessed he knew.

Tadd was trying to peer inside. "Mom, I can't see," he whispered loudly in irritation.

Bending down, Valerie lifted him up. His arm rested on her shoulder, his face close to her own. "That's your great-grandfather." She felt the need to tell him something.

"Gee!" Tadd breathed, and turned a

questioning scowl on her. "How come we didn't bury Fred in a box like that?" he asked loudly.

A smile played at the edges of her mouth. His nonchalance at death seemed somehow right. She wasn't going to scold him for being disrespectful.

"We couldn't find one that small," she answered, and it satisfied him.

As they turned to walk back to where the other mourners were talking, Judd gave her a questioning look, his eyes cool and distant. "Who's Fred?"

"A pet turtle," she admitted, unable to keep from giving him a faint smile.

"I should have guessed," he murmured dryly, shared amusement glittering briefly in his look.

More friends of the family arrived. Judd made no attempt to remain at her side as Valerie greeted them. Almost immediately he drifted to one side, although Valerie was aware that he was never very far away from her.

It wasn't long before the newness of Tadd's surroundings wore off. He became increasingly restless and impatient with the subdued conversations. He fidgeted in the folding chair beside Valerie's and began violently swinging his feet back and forth to kick at his chair rung. The clatter of his shoes against the metal was loud, like a galloping horse.

"Don't do that, Tadd," Valerie told him quietly, putting a hand on his knee to end the motion.

He flashed her a defiant look that said "I want to" and continued swinging his feet without letup.

"Stop it, Tadd," she repeated.

"No!" he retorted in open belligerence, and found himself looking into a pair of cold green eyes that wouldn't put up with such rebellion.

"Do as your mother tells you, Tadd," Judd warned, "or you'll find yourself sitting alone in your mother's car."

Tadd pushed his mutinous face close to Judd's. "Good." Olive green eyes glared into a brilliant jade green pair. "I want to sit in the car," Tadd declared. "I don't want to stay here in this dumb old place."

"Very well." Judd straightened, taking one of Tadd's hands and pulling him from the chair.

"No, wait." Valerie rushed out the halting words. "Tadd is tired and irritable after that long trip," she explained to excuse her son's behavior, and glanced anxiously at Clara. "Maybe you'd better take him back and put him to bed, Clara." She opened her bag and took out the car keys. "Here."

"And how will you get back?" her friend challenged in a meaningful voice.

It didn't seem proper to Valerie to leave yet. Mickey Flanners was standing only a few feet away, chatting with a horse trainer.

"Mickey?" When he turned, Valerie asked, "Is it all right if I ride back to the farm with you?"

For an instant she thought Mickey glanced at Judd before answering, but she decided she had been mistaken. "Sure," he agreed immediately.

Judd released Tadd's hand as Clara walked over to take him with her. Tadd glanced at Valerie. "I'll be there soon," she promised.

It was more than an hour later when Mickey asked if she was ready to leave. Valerie agreed and was required to say no more as Mickey began relating a steady stream of racehorse gossip while they walked out of the funeral home. Only one car was parked in the area that Mickey was heading toward, and Judd was behind the wheel.

"Where are you parked?" Valerie interrupted Mickey with the question.

"I thought you knew." His startled glance

was strictly innocent of deception. "I rode in with Judd."

"No, I wasn't aware of that." There was a hint of grimness in her voice, but she didn't protest.

Mickey opened the front door on the passenger side for her. She had barely slid in when he was asking her to move over. She found herself sitting in the middle, pressed close to Judd. For such a small man, Mickey Flanners seemed to take up a lot of room.

Judd appeared indifferent to the way her shoulder kept brushing against his as he reversed the car into the street. It was impossible to avoid the accidental contact with him unless she hunched her shoulders forward and held herself as stiffly as an old woman, and she refused to do that.

The expensive scent of male cologne filled her lungs and interfered with her breathing. Mickey continued his nonstop banter, which was a source of relief to Valerie, for without it she was certain Judd would have been able to hear the erratic pounding of her heart.

When Judd had to swerve the car to avoid a pothole, Valerie was thrown against him. Her hand clutched at the nearest solid object to regain her balance. It turned out to be his thigh. His muscles contracted into living steel beneath her hand. She heard him sharply inhale a curse and jerked her hand away as if she had suddenly been burned.

She recovered enough of her poise to offer a cool, "I'm sorry."

His bland, "That's quite all right," made her wonder if she had only imagined that he had been disturbed by her unconsciously intimate touch.

Her grandfather's house was a welcome sight when Judd slowed the car to a stop in front of it. Mickey didn't immediately climb out. Instead he leaned forward to take a look at Judd.

"There's some of Eli's good brandy in the house. Will you come in, Judd, and we'll have one last drink to old Eli?" A second after he had issued the invitation he glanced at Valerie. "That is, if you don't mind. After all, it is your grandfather's house and his brandy."

"It's as much your house as it is mine," Valerie insisted. What else could she say? Mickey had worked for her grandfather long before she was born. His years of loyalty far outweighed her less than exemplary relationship with her grandfather, regardless of the blood ties.

"In that case, will you come in for a little

while, Judd?" Mickey repeated his invitation.

There was an instant's hesitation from Judd. Valerie felt his gaze skim her profile, but she pretended obliviousness to the look. She hadn't seconded the invitation because she didn't want to give him the impression that she desired his company. Neither did she seek to avoid it because she didn't want him to know he still exerted a powerful attraction over her.

"Thank you, Mick, I'd like that," he agreed finally. "But I'll only be able to stay a little while. I've got a sick colt to check on."

"Oh? What's wrong with it?" Mick opened his car door and stepped out.

As Valerie partially turned to slide out the passenger side, the skirt of her grape-colored dress failed to move with her, exposing a sheer nylon-covered thigh and knee. She reached hastily to pull the skirt down, but Judd's hand was there to do it for her. In the confusion of his touch against her virtually bare leg, Valerie didn't hear his explanation of the colt's problem. She managed to push his hand away, an action that was at odds with her sensual reaction.

The warmth that was in her cheeks when she stepped out of the car wasn't visible in the fading sunset of the summer evening. It was a languid night, heavily scented with the smell of horses and hay and a sprinkling of roses that grew next to the house.

Mickey waited for Judd to continue his discussion of horses and their ailments. Valerie started immediately toward the house, not rushing her pace as one would in fleeing, although that was what she wanted to do. In consequence, Judd was there to reach around her and open the porch door.

Hearing them return, Clara appeared from the living room. She had already changed into her nightgown, its hem peeping out from the folds of her quilted robe. A pair of furry slippers covered her feet. At the sight of the two men following Valerie inside, Clara stopped and scowled. Only Valerie, who knew her, was aware it was a self-conscious and defensive expression for being caught in that state of dress.

"What are you staring at?" Clara demanded of Mickey in her most rasping and abrasive voice. "Haven't you ever seen a woman in a bathrobe before?"

"Not in a good many years." Mickey recovered from his initial shock, his cheeks dimpling with mischief. "I'd forgotten what a tempting sight it could be."

"Watch your tongue!" Clara snapped, reddening under his sweeping look.

Hiding a grin, Mickey turned aside from the bristling woman. "I'll get some glasses from the kitchen. Why don't you go on into Eli's office, Judd? I'll be along directly."

"Don't rush on my account," Judd replied.

Valerie felt his glance swing to her when Mickey left the room, but she didn't volunteer to show him to her grandfather's office/study. Instead she walked into the living room to speak to Clara, denying any interest in where he went or when.

"Is Tadd asleep?" she asked Clara.

"Finally, after throwing a holy fit to see the horses again," was the gruff response.

"I'll go and look in on him." Her sensitive radar knew the instant Judd turned and walked toward the study.

"Leave him be for now," Clara insisted. "You might wake him, and I don't care to hear him whining again about those horses." She shot a look in the direction Judd had taken and whispered angrily, "You could have warned me you'd be inviting them in when you got back. I wouldn't have been traipsing around the place in my robe if I'd known."

"I had no intention of inviting them in," Valerie corrected. "In fact, Mickey was the one who invited Judd, not me."

"It's neither here nor there now," Clara muttered. "I'm going up to my room where I can have some privacy."

Valerie was about to say that she'd come along with her when Mickey appeared at the living room entrance. Clara scurried toward the staircase under his dancing look.

"I'll be up shortly," she called after Clara, then asked Mickey, "Did you want something?"

"I know you're tired and will be wanting to turn in, but will you have one small drink with us to the old man?" He wore his most beguiling expression as he raised an arm to show her he carried three glasses.

The haunting loneliness in his blue eyes told Valerie that he truly missed her grandfather and wanted to share his sense of loss with someone who had been close to Elias Wentworth. Her glance flickered uncertainly toward the study where Judd waited.

"Very well," she agreed, and wondered whether she was a sentimental fool or a masochist.

Judd's back was to the door, his attention focused on the framed pictures of thoroughbred horses that covered one paneled wall of the study. Valerie tried not to notice the way he pivoted sharply when she and Mickey entered, or the almost physical thrust of his gaze on her. She walked to the leather-covered armchair, its dark brown color worn to patches of tan on the seat and arms.

"I've got the glasses," Mickey announced. "All we need is the brandy." He walked to the stained oak desk and opened a bottom drawer. "Up until a few years ago Eli used to keep his liquor locked up in the safe."

Valerie's fingers curved into the leather armrest at Mickey's unwitting reminder of her past misdeeds. Her grandfather had kept it locked away to prevent her from drinking it. To this day, she didn't understand why she had done it. She hadn't liked the taste of alcohol and had usually ended up getting sick.

"Eli never touched a drop himself," Mickey went on as he held the bottle up to see how much was in it. "He was an alcoholic when he was younger. He told me once that it wasn't until after his wife died that he gave up drinking for good." He poured a healthy amount of brandy into the first water glass.

"Only a little for me," said Valerie, understanding at last why her grandfather had been so violently opposed to drinking.

"Eli swore he kept liquor in the house purely for medicinal reasons." When he reached the third glass, Mickey poured only enough brandy in to cover the bottom. "Personally, I think he kept it on hand to befuddle the brains of whoever came to buy a horse from him."

Picking up two of the glasses, Mickey carried the one with the smallest portion to Valerie and handed the other to Judd. Judd took a seat on the worn leather-covered sofa that was a match to her chair. Mickey completed the triangle by hoisting himself onto the desk top, his short legs dangling against the side.

"To Eli." Judd lifted his glass in a toast.

"May he rest in peace," Mickey added, and drank from his glass. Valerie sipped her brandy, the fiery liquid burning her tongue and throat, conscious that Judd's gaze seldom wavered from her. "Yeah, old Eli never smoked or drank," Mickey sighed, and stared at his glass. "They say a reformed hellion is stricter — and he sure was with you, Valerie. I remember the time he caught you with a pack of cigarettes. I thought he was going to beat the livin' tar out of you."

"I caused him a lot of grief when I was growing up." She lifted her shoulders in a dismissing shrug.

"You were a chip off the old block," the

ex-jockey insisted with a smile, countering her self-criticism. "Besides, you gave him a lot of pleasure these last years." His comment warmed her. "Remember how Eli was, Judd, whenever he got a letter from her?"

"Yes," Judd answered quietly.

At his affirmative reply, her gaze swung curiously to him. "Did you visit granddad? I don't remember that you came over when I was still living here."

He rotated his glass in a circle, swirling the brandy inside. He seemed to be pretending an interest in the liquor while choosing how to word his answer.

"Your grandfather had a yearling filly that I liked the looks of a few years ago. Her bloodline wasn't bad, so I offered to buy her," Judd explained with a touch of diffidence. "After a week of haggling back and forth, we finally came to an agreement on the price. It was the first time I really became acquainted with Eli. I like to think that we had a mutual respect for each other."

"After that, Judd began stopping by once or twice a month," Mickey elaborated. "Your granddad would get out his letters from you and tell anybody who would listen how you were."

Apprehension quivered through Valerie that Judd might have seen what she wrote. Of course, she had never told her grandfather the identity of Tadd's father, not even in the letters. Not that she cared whether Judd knew, but she didn't like the idea that he might have read the personal letters intended only for her grandfather. Mickey's next statement put that apprehension to rest.

"He never actually read your letters aloud, but he'd tell what you said. All the time he'd be talking, he'd be holding the envelope with your letter inside it and stroking it like it was one of his horses."

"I wish . . . I could have seen him before he died." But she hadn't thought she would be welcomed.

"I wanted to call you when he was in the hospital," Mickey told her. "But Eli told me that in your last letter you'd said you and your husband were going to take a Caribbean cruise. I didn't know he was so sick or I would have got in touch with you anyway."

"On a cruise?" Valerie frowned.

"That's what he said," Mickey repeated.

"I didn't go on any cruise," she denied before she realized that it was another story her grandfather had made up.

"Maybe he got your letters confused," he

suggested. "He kept them all, every one of them. He hoarded them like they were gold. He carried them around with him until they stuck out of the pockets of his old green plaid jacket like straw out of a scarecrow."

"He did?" Valerie was bemused by the thought. The idea that he treasured her letters that much made her forgive him for making up those stories about her.

"He sure did. As a matter of fact, they're all still in his jacket." Mickey hopped down from his perch on the desk and walked to the old armoire used as a storage cabinet for the farm records. The green plaid jacket hung on a hook inside the wooden door. "Here it is, letters and all."

As he walked over to her, Mickey began gathering the letters from the various pockets, not stopping until there were several handfuls on her lap. Some of the envelopes had the yellow tinge of age, but all of them were worn from numerous handlings.

Setting her brandy glass down, Valerie picked up one envelope that was postmarked five years ago. She turned it over, curious to read the letter inside, but the flap of the envelope was still sealed. A cold chill raced through her.

"No!" Her cry was a sobbing protest of angry and hurt disbelief. She raced frantically through the rest of the envelopes. All were sealed. None of the letters had ever been read. "No! No! No!" She sobbed out bitter, futile denials of a truth too painful to accept.

"What is it?" Mickey was plainly confused.

"What's wrong?" Judd was standing beside her chair. He reached down and took one of the envelopes.

"Look at it!" Valerie challenged through her tears.

When he turned it over and saw the sealed flap that had no marks of ever having been opened, his darkly green, questing gaze sliced back to her. In each of her hands she held envelopes in the same unopened condition. Her fingers curled into them, crumpling them into her palms. In agitation she rose from the chair, letting the letters in her lap fall to the floor. She stared at the ones in her hands.

"It isn't fair!" In a mixture of rage and pain, Valerie cast away the envelopes in her hands. She began shaking uncontrollably, her fingers still curled into fists. "It isn't fair!"

Scalding tears burned hot trails down her cheeks. The emotion-charged feelings and tempers maturity had taught her to control broke free of the restraints to erupt in a stormy display.

"Valerie!" Judd's quieting voice had the opposite effect.

The instant his hands gripped her shoulders and turned her around, she began pummeling his shoulders with her fists. Sobbing in earnest, she was like the tigress he had once called her, with tawny hair and topaz eyes, wounded and lashing out from the hurt.

"He never opened them. He never read any of my letters," she sobbed in frustration and anguish.

Indifferent to the hands on her waist, she pounded Judd's shoulders, hitting out at the only solid object in the vicinity. Her crying face was buried in his shirtfront, moistening it and the lapel of his jacket.

Somewhere on the edge of her consciousness she was aware of concerned voices, Mickey's and Clara's. Only one penetrated and it came from Judd.

"Let her cry. She needs the release."

After that, there was only silence and the heart-tearing sounds of her own sobbing. When the violence within subsided, she cried softly for several minutes more. Her hands stopped beating at the indestructible wall of muscle and clutched the expensive material of Judd's jacket instead. His arms were around her, holding her closely in silent comfort. Gradually she began to regain her senses, but there were still things that needed to come out.

Lifting her head far enough from his chest to see the buttons of his shirt, she sniffed, "He hated me." Her voice was hoarse and broken as she wiped the wetness from her cheek with a scrubbing motion of her hand.

"I'm sure he didn't," Judd denied.

"Yes, he did." Valerie bobbed her head, a caramel curtain of rippling hair failing forward to hide her face. "He couldn't stand the thought of having me as a granddaughter, so he made up a fictitious one, complete with stories about marriage and vacation cruises. It was all lies!"

His hand raked the hair from one cheek and tilted her face up for his glittering study. "What are you saying?" he demanded with tight-lipped grimness.

Golden defiance flashed in her eyes, a defiance for convention and her grandfather. "I work for a living. I couldn't afford a trip on a rowboat. I'm not married — I never have been. Tadd is his great-grandchild, but without the legitimacy of a marriage license."

"Damn you!" His head came down, his

mouth roughly brushing across a tear-dampened cheek to reach her lips. "I've been going through hell wondering how I was going to keep my hands off somebody else's wife." He breathed the savagely issued words into her mouth. "And all the time you weren't even married!"

The hungry ferocity of his kiss claimed her lips, devouring their fullness. Her battered emotions had no defenses against his rapacious assault and he fed on her weakness. She was dragged into the powerful undercurrent of his passion, then swept high by the response of her own senses. The flames of carnal longing licked through her veins to heat her flesh. This consuming fire fused her melting curves to the iron contours of his male form. Not content with the domination of her lips, Judd ravaged her throat and the sensitive hollows below her ears.

His hand moved slowly down her back, unzipping her dress, but when the room's air touched the exposed skin, it was the cool breath of sanity that she had needed. She pushed out of his arms and took a quick step away, stopping with her back to him. She was trembling from the force of the passion he had so easily aroused.

At the touch of his hand on her hair, Valerie stiffened. Judd brushed the long toffee mane of hair aside. His warm breath caressed her skin as he bent to kiss the ultrasensitive spot at the back of her neck, and desire quivered through her.

"You're right, Valerie." His fingers teased her spine as he zipped up her dress. "This isn't the time nor the place, not with your grandfather's funeral tomorrow."

"As if you give a damn!" Her voice wavered under the burning weight of resentment and bitterness. She dredged up the parting phrase she had used seven years ago. "Go to hell, Judd Prescott!"

She closed her eyes tightly as she heard his footsteps recede from her. When she opened them they were dry of tears and she was alone. A few minutes later Clara came slopping into the room in her furry slippers.

"Are you all right now?" she questioned.

Valerie turned, breathing in deeply and nodding a curt, "Yes, I'm fine." The letters were still scattered on the linoleum floor, and she stooped to pick them up. "Granddad never opened them, Clara."

"That doesn't mean anything. He kept them, didn't he? So he must have felt something for you," her friend reasoned, "otherwise he would have burned them."

"Maybe." But Valerie was no longer sure.

"What did Prescott have to say?" Clara

bent awkwardly down on her knees to help Valerie collect the scattered envelopes.

"Nothing really. I told him I wasn't married and that Tadd was illegitimate, so he knows granddad was lying all this time," she replied with almost frightening calm.

"Did you tell him he was Tadd's father? Is that why he left in such a freezing silence?"

"No. He never asked who Tadd's father was. I'm just a tramp to him. I doubt if he even believes I know who the father is," she said, releasing a short bitter laugh. The postmark of one of the envelopes in her hand caught her eye. It was dated two days after Tadd's birth, unopened like the rest of them. "If granddad never opened any of my letters, how did he know about Tadd?"

Clara stood up, making a show of straightening the stack of envelopes she held. "I phoned him a couple hours after Tadd was born. I thought he should know he had a great-grandson."

"What . . . did he say?" Valerie unconsciously held her breath.

Clara hesitated, then looked her in the eye. "He didn't say anything. He just hung up." The flickering light of hope went out of Valerie's eyes. "I was talking to Mickey today," Clara went on. "It wasn't until a year after Tadd was born that he told everybody he had a great-grandchild."

"I suppose so there was a decent interval between the time I supposedly was married and Tadd was born," Valerie concluded acidly. "Damn!" she swore softly and with pain. "Now all of them think Tadd is five years old instead of six."

"I know it hurts." Clara's brisk voice tried to offer comfort. "But, in his way, I think your grandfather was trying to keep people from talking bad about you."

"I'm not going to live his lies!" Valerie flashed.

"You don't have to, but I wouldn't suggest going around broadcasting the truth, either," the other woman cautioned. "You might be able to thumb your nose at the gossip you'd start, but there's Tadd to consider."

Valerie released a long breath in silent acknowledgement of her logic. "Where's Mickey?" she asked.

"He went out to the barn, said there was a place for him to sleep there where he could be close to the horses," Clara answered.

"I'm tired, too." Valerie felt emotionally drained, her energy sapped. Exhaustion was stealing through her limbs. She handed the letters to Clara, not caring what she did with them, and walked toward the stairs.

CHAPTER FOUR

A bee buzzed lazily around the wreath of flowers lying on the coffin and a green canopy shaded the mourners from the glare of the sun. Valerie absently watched the bee's wanderings. Her attention had strayed from the intoning voice of the minister.

At the "Amen," she lifted her gaze and encountered Judd's steady regard. Her pulse altered its regular tempo before she glanced away. The graveside service was over and the minister was approaching her. Valerie smiled politely and thanked him, words and gestures that she repeated to several others until she was facing Judd.

"It was good of you to come." She offered him the same stilted phrase.

His carved bronze features were expressionless as he inclined his head in smooth acknowledgement. A dancing breeze combed its fingers through his black hair as he drew her attention to the woman at his side, ushering her forward.

"I don't believe you've met my mother, Valerie," he said. "This is Valerie Wentworth." An inbred old-world courtesy prompted him to introduce the younger to the elder first. "My mother, Maureen Prescott."

"How do you do, Mrs. Prescott." Valerie shook the white-gloved hand, her gaze curiously skimming the woman who had given birth to this man.

Petitely built, she had black hair with startling wings of silver at the temples. Her eyes were an unusual shade of turquoise green, not as brilliant as her son's nor as disconcerting. She was attractive, her face generally unlined. She conveyed warmth where her son revealed cynicism. Valerie decided that Maureen Prescott was a genteel woman made of flexible steel.

"Judd was better acquainted with your grandfather than I, but please accept my sincere sympathies," the woman offered in a pleasant, gentle voice.

"Thank you." Valerie thawed slightly.

"If there's anything you need, please remember that we're your neighbors." A smile curved the perfectly shaped lips.

"I will, Mrs. Prescott," she nodded, knowing it was the last place she would go for assistance.

Others were waiting to speak to her and Judd didn't attempt to prolong the exchange with her. As he walked his mother toward the line of cars parked along the cemetery gates, Valerie's gaze strayed after them, following their progress.

When the last of those waiting approached her, Valerie almost sighed aloud. The strain of hearing the same words and repeating the same phrases in answer was beginning to wear on her nerves.

She offered the man her hand. "It was kind of you to come," she recited.

"I'm Jefferson Burrows," he said, as if the name was supposed to mean something to her. Valerie looked at him without recognition. He was of medium height, in his early fifties, and carried himself with a certain air of authority. "I was your grandfather's attorney," he explained.

"I'm pleased to meet you, Mr. Burrows." She kept hold of her fraying patience.

"This is not perhaps the proper time, but I was wondering if I might arrange to see you tomorrow," he said.

"I'll probably be fairly busy tomorrow. You see, I stored many of my personal things at my grandfather's, childhood mementoes, et cetera," she explained coolly. "I planned to sort through them tomorrow and I'll be leaving the day after to return to Cincinnati. Was it important?"

"I do need to go over your grandfather's

will with you before you leave." There was a hint of pomposity that she had implied he had made a request that was not important.

"There's a provision for me in his will?" Her response was incredulous and skeptical.

"Naturally, as his only living relative, you are one of the beneficiaries of his estate." His tone was reprimanding. "May I call in the morning? Around ten o'clock, perhaps?"

"Yes. Yes, that will be fine." Valerie felt a bit dazed.

As she and Mickey drove away from the cemetery a short time later, she saw the attorney standing beside the Prescott car talking to Judd. After having previously been convinced that she would be disinherited, Valerie had difficulty adjusting to the fact that her grandfather had left a bequest for her in his will.

It was even more difficult for her to accept the next morning after Jefferson Burrows read her the will. She stared at the paper listing assets and liabilities belonging to her grandfather and the approximate net worth of the estate. All of it, except for a cash amount to Mickey, had been left to her.

"You do understand," the attorney said, "that the values on the breeding stock and the farm are approximate market prices, but I've been conservative in fixing them. Also, this figure doesn't take into account the amount of tax you'll have to pay. Do you have any questions?"

"No." How could she tell him she was overwhelmed just at the thought of inheriting?

"You're fortunate that your grandfather wasn't one to incur a lot of debts. The only sizable one is the mortgage on the farm."

"Yes, I am." Valerie tried to answer with some degree of poise.

"I know this inheritance doesn't represent a large sum of money," he said, and she wondered what he used as a standard of measure. There was money for Tadd's education and enough left over that she wouldn't have to work for a year if she didn't want to. "But I'm sure you'll want to discuss it with your husband before you make any decision about possibly disposing of the property."

"I'm not married, Mr. Burrows." She corrected his misconception immediately.

He raised an eyebrow at that, but made no direct comment. "In that case, perhaps I should go over some of the alternatives with you. Deducting taxes and the bequest to Mr. Flanners, there isn't sufficient working capital to keep the farm running. Of course, you could borrow against your assets to obtain the capital, but in doing so, you would be jeopardizing all of what you inherited."

"Yes, I can see that," Valerie agreed, and she didn't like the idea of risking Tadd's future education.

"I would advise that you auction all the horses to eliminate an immediate drain on your limited resources and to either lease or sell the land." He began going into more detail, discussing the pros and cons of each possibility until Valerie's mind was spinning in confusion. It was a relief when he began shoving the legal papers into his briefcase. "It isn't necessary that you make an immediate decision. In fact, I recommend that you think about it for a week or two before letting me know which course of action you would like to pursue."

"Yes, I'll do that." She would need that much time to sort through all the advice he had given her.

After he had gone, she broke the good news to Clara, but even then it didn't really sink in. It wasn't until after lunch when the dishes were done and she and Tadd and Clara had walked outside that the full import of it struck her.

Valerie looked out over the pastures, the grazing mares and colts, the stables and barns, and the house, and she was dazzled by what she saw.

"It's mine, Clara," she murmured. "I inherited all of this. It's really and truly mine."

"Do you mean it's yours like the car is?" Tadd asked, sensing the importance of her statement, but not understanding its implications.

"The car belongs to me and the bank," Valerie corrected him with a bright smile. "I guess the bank has a piece of this, too, but I have a bigger one."

"Does that mean we can live here?" His eyes rounded at the thought.

"We could live here if we wanted to," she agreed without thinking, since it was one of the choices.

"You're forgetting you have a job to go to in Cincinnati," Clara inserted dryly.

"I'm not forgetting." Valerie shook her head, then turned her bright gaze on the older woman. "Don't you see, Clara, I have enough money that I could quit my job?"

"Now you're beginning to sound like some heiress," observed Clara in a puncturing tone.

"I wouldn't be able to quit working forever," Valerie conceded, "but there's enough money here for Tadd to have a college education and to support us for a whole year besides."

"Are we really going to live here, mommy?" Tadd was almost dancing with excitement.

"I don't know yet, honey," she told him.

"I want to. Please, can we live here?" he asked breathlessly.

"We'll talk about it later," Valerie stalled. "You run off and play now. Don't go near the horses, though, unless Mickey is with you," she called as he went dashing off.

"You shouldn't be raising the boy's hopes up," Clara reprimanded. "You know you can't live here permanently."

"Maybe not permanently, but we could stay here through the summer." At the scoffing sound, Valerie outlined the idea that had been germinating in her mind. "It would be a vacation, the first time I'd be able to be with Tadd for more than just nights and weekends. And I'd like him to know the freedom of country life."

"What would you do with yourself out here?" Clara wanted to know.

"There's a lot that could be done. First, the horses would all have to be auctioned. And Mr. Burrows suggested that I might get a better price for the farm if I invested some money in painting the buildings and fences. The lawn would need to be cleaned up and maintained. There's something to be gained from staying the summer. Besides, it would take time to sell or lease the place," she reasoned. "What are we talking about anyway? Just two and a half or three months."

"What about your job? You are supposed to be back to work on Friday," Clara reminded her.

"I know," Valerie admitted. "I'll just have to see if Mr. Hanover will give me leave of absence until the fall."

"And if he won't?"

"Then I'll have to find another job." Valerie refused to regard this point as an obstacle. "This time I'll have enough money to support myself until I find a good one."

"It seems to me you have your mind all made up," Clara sniffed, as if offended that her counsel hadn't been sought.

"The more I think about it, the more I like it," Valerie admitted. "You could stay, too, Clara. The doctor said you had to rest for a month. Why not here in the fresh air and sunshine?"

"If you're set on staying here, I might, too." There was something grudging in the reply. "I'm just not sure in my mind that you're doing the right thing."

"Give me one good reason for not staying the summer," Valerie demanded with a challenging smile.

"Judd Prescott." The answer was quick and sure.

The smile was wiped from Valerie's face as if it had never been there. "He has nothing to do with my decision!" she snapped, her eyes flashing yellow sparks.

"Maybe he doesn't, but he's someone you're going to have to contend with," Clara retorted. "And soon, it appears." Her eyes narrowed, gazing in the direction of the pasture beyond Valerie.

Hearing the drum of galloping hooves, Valerie turned to see a big gray hunter approaching the yard. The rider was instantly recognizable as Judd. Alertness splintered through her senses, putting her instantly on guard.

Tossing its head, the gray horse was reined in at the board fence. Judd dismounted and looped the reins around the upright post. He crossed the board fence and walked toward the two women with ease that said it was a commonplace thing for him to be stopping by. His arrogant assumption that he would be welcomed rankled Valerie.

"What do you want, Mr. Prescott?" She coldly attempted to put him in his place as an uninvited trespasser.

His hard mouth curved into a smile that lacked both humor and warmth as he stopped before her. "I have some business that I want to discuss with you, *Miss* Wentworth." Sardonically he mocked her formality.

"What business would that be?" she challenged, her chin lifting.

His gaze skimmed her once over, taking in the crisp Levi's and the light blue print of her cotton blouse. His look belied his previous statement that his purpose was business, not personal.

"I understand that Mr. Burrows was here to see you this morning," he replied without answering her question.

"And where did you get that piece of information?" Valerie demanded.

"From Mr. Burrows," Judd answered complacently. His mouth twisted briefly at the flash of indignation in her look. "I asked him to call me after he'd informed you of your inheritance."

"Just what do you know about my inheritance?" She was practically seething at the attorney's lack of confidentiality.

"That your grandfather left everything to you."

"I suppose Mr. Burrows supplied you with that information, too." Irritation put a razor-sharp edge to her tightly controlled voice.

"No, your grandfather did," Judd smoothly corrected her assumption.

"I see," she said stiffly. "Now that we have that straightened out, what did you want?"

"As I said, I have some business to discuss with you regarding your inheritance." His gaze flicked to the onlooking Clara. "In private."

"There isn't anything you have to say to me that I would object to having Clara hear," Valerie stated.

"But *I* object," Judd countered. "If you want to discuss my proposal with Clara after I'm gone, that's your business, Valerie. But my business is with you and you alone, with no third party listening in."

Valerie held her breath and counted to ten. Was it really business he wanted to discuss or was it some trick to get her alone? There was nothing in his expression to tell her the answer.

"Very well," she agreed, however ungraciously. "Shall we walk, Mr. Prescott? Then you won't have to worry about anyone eavesdropping on your so very private business conversation."

"By all means let's walk." Amusement glittered in his eyes at her sarcasm.

Valerie started off in the direction of the pasture fence where the gray hunter was tied. When they had traveled what she considered a sufficient distance, she glanced at him.

"Is this far enough?" she questioned.

He glanced over his shoulder at Clara, a taunting light in his eyes when their gaze returned to Valerie. "For the time being," he agreed.

"Then perhaps you would be good enough to state your business." Her nerves felt as tight as a drum and the pounding of her heart increased the sensation.

"I don't know if you have had time to decide what you want to do about the farm, whether you're going to keep it or sell it," Judd began without hesitation. "I'm willing to pay whatever the market price is for the farm if you decide to sell."

So it was business, she realized, and was angered by the disappointment she felt. "I see." She couldn't think of anything else to say.

"I offered to buy the place from your grandfather, but he wouldn't sell. It isn't a money-making concern, Valerie," he warned. "Your grandfather has a good stallion in Sunnybrook, but his mares are less than desirable. I tried to convince him that he should be more selective in the mares he bred to the stallion, but he needed the stud fees and couldn't afford to buy better-bred mares."

But Valerie's thoughts had strayed to another area. "Why did granddad tell you he was leaving all this to me?"

His gaze narrowed with wicked suggestion. "Do you mean did he know that you and I were once lovers?" She hadn't expected him to word her suspicion so bluntly. The uncomfortable rush of color to her cheeks angered her. Turning her back on Judd, she walked to the pasture fence, closing her hands over the edge of the top rail.

"Did he guess?" she demanded, letting him know that she had never told her grandfather.

"No. If he had, he'd probably have chased me off his land with a load of buckshot," he answered.

"I . . . wondered," Valerie offered in a weak explanation for her question.

"You look more like the Valerie I remember, standing there with your lion's mane of shiny hair around your shoulders and those tight-fitting jeans that show off your perfectly rounded bottom."

If he had stripped her on the spot, Valerie couldn't have felt more naked. She pivoted around to face him, hiding the area he had described with such knowledge from his roaming gaze. Leaning against the fence, she hooked the heel of one boot on the lowest rail.

"I think you said it was business you wanted to discuss," she reminded him with flashing temper.

He looked amused. "Have you given any thought to selling?"

Despite his compliance with her challenge, Valerie didn't feel much safer. "I'm considering it . . . as well as several other possibilities."

"Such as staying on here permanently?" he suggested.

"I don't think that's possible," she said, rejecting that idea with a brief shake of her head. "As you mentioned, the horses barely pay for themselves, so it would be difficult for me to earn a living from the farm."

"You could always sell the horses and lease all the land except the house." Judd took a step toward the fence, but he was angled away from her, posing no threat.

"I could," Valerie conceded, "but the

income from a lease wouldn't be enough to support us. I'd need a job and there aren't many openings for a secretary in this community, especially well-paying ones. It's too far to commute to Baltimore. For that reason leasing practically cancels itself out."

"Don't be too certain that you wouldn't have enough money from a lease," he cautioned. "The right party might be willing to pay what you need."

He began wandering along the fence row, gazing out over the land as if appraising its worth. Valerie watched him, confused by the possibility he had raised. She didn't know whether he was telling her the truth or dangling a carrot under her nose to lead her into a trap. Or had there been a hidden suggestion in his words that she hadn't caught?

Before she could puzzle it out, Judd was asking, "Do you mind if we walk on a little farther?" His sideways look of question held a bemused light. "I'd like to get out from underneath the eagle eye of that battle-ax."

"Do you mean Clara?" Valerie was startled but not offended by his mocking reference to her friend. Without being aware of moving she began following him, matching his strolling pace.

"Yes," he admitted. "She reminds me of one of those buxom warrior maids in a

German opera. All she lacks are pigtails, a spear and an armored breastplate."

Valerie visualized Clara in such a costume and couldn't help smiling at the image and the aptness of his description. "Does she make you uncomfortable?" she asked.

Judd stopped, his level gaze swinging to her with a force that rooted her to the ground. "You make me uncomfortable, Valerie."

His hand lifted, the back of his fingers stroking the line of her jaw before she could elude them. The light touch was destroying. When his fingertips traced the length of the sensitive cord in her neck all the way to the hollow of her throat, her breath was stolen by the traitorous awakening of her senses. She sank her white teeth into the softness of her lower lip to hold back the words trembling on her tongue, unsure whether they would come out a protest or an invitation.

Taking her silence as acceptance, Judd moved closer. He hooked a finger under the collar of her blouse and followed its line to the lowest point where a button blocked his way, but not for long. A languorous warmth spread over her skin when his hand slid inside her blouse to climb and claim the rosy mountain of her breast. He bent his head to kiss the lip her teeth held captive, and they abandoned it to his sensual inspection. Her heart throbbed with aching force under his sweet mastery. Inflamed by his slow burning fire, Valerie trembled with passion.

Satisfied with her initial response, Judd began nuzzling her cheek and eye, his tongue sending shivers of raw desire through her as it licked her ear. The heady male smell of him stimulated her already churning emotions. Of their own free will, her lips were nibbling and kissing the strong, smooth line of his jaw.

"I'll lease the place from you, Valerie," Judd muttered against her cheek, "and pay you whatever you need to live on."

His offer stopped her heartbeat. "Would you visit me?" she whispered, wanting to be sure she hadn't misunderstood.

"Regularly." His massaging hand tightened possessively on her breast as he gathered her more fully into his encircling hold. He sought the corner of her lips, his warm breath mingling with hers. "Night and day."

With shattering clarity, his true proposition was brought home to her. Leasing the land was only a means to give her money — money that would oblige her to be available whenever he felt the urge for her company. She inwardly reeled from the thought with pain and bitterness.

Her lips escaped his smothering kiss long enough to ask chokingly, "Would the lease be . . . long-term or . . . short?"

"Any terms, I don't care." Impatience edged his voice. "After seven years, I want to make love to you very slowly, but you drive me to the edge of control," he muttered thickly, his mouth making another foray to her neck.

Sickened by the weakness that made her thrill to his admission, Valerie lowered her head to escape his insatiable kisses and strained her hands against his chest to gain breathing room. Judd didn't object. It was as if he knew how easily he could subdue any major show of resistance from her. This arrogance was the whip to flog her into a cold anger.

"I'll tell you what my terms are, Judd." She lifted her head slowly, keeping her lashes lowered to conceal the hard, topaz glitter in her eyes until she was ready for him to see it. "My terms are —" she paused, taking one last look at her fingers spread across his powerful chest before lifting her gaze to his face "— no terms."

As his green eyes began to narrow at her expression, she struck with feline swiftness. Her open palm lashed across his cheek in a stinging report, to be immediately caught in the viselike grip of his fingers.

"I won't lease you the land, the buildings, or my body," she hissed. "I will not become your consort!"

She tried twisting her wrist out of his hold, but Judd wrapped it behind her back. Her other hand met the same fate and she was completely trapped in the steel circle of his arms. Deliberately he ground her hips against his, making her aware of his aroused state, which had nothing to do with the anger blazing in his expression.

"You spitting little hellcat," he jeered. "You haven't changed. Seven years may have given you a certain amount of poise and sophistication, but underneath you're the same passionate and untamed she-devil. You want me to make love to you as much as I do."

"No!" Valerie rushed the vigorous denial.

His upper lip curled into a taunting smile as if he knew how hollow her denial was. "Yes, you do," he insisted with infuriating complacency, and let her go. "Sooner or later you'll admit it."

Turning away smoothly, he began walking toward his horse, leaving Valerie standing there with a mouthful of angry words. She ran after him, trembling with rage.

"You'll rot in hell before I do," she told him in a voice shaking with violence.

His green eyes flashed her a lazy, mocking look before he slipped between the rails of the board fence with an ease that belied his six-foot frame and muscled build. The tall gray horse whickered as he approached. Valerie stopped, staying on the opposite side of the fence, her hands doubled into impotent fists.

Unhooking the reins from the post, Judd looped them around the horse's neck and swung into the saddle with an expert grace. The big gray bunched its hindquarters, eager to be off at the first command from its rider, but none came. Judd looked down at Valerie from his high vantage point in the saddle.

"I meant it when I said I wanted to buy this place," he said flatly. "If you decide to sell, I want you to know my interest in purchasing it is purely a business one. No other consideration will enter into the negotiations for the price."

"I'm glad to hear it." She struggled to control her temper and sounded cold as a result. "Because any offer from you with strings attached will be rejected out of hand!"

His half smile implied that he believed

differently. If there had been anything within reach, Valerie would have thrown it at him. Before she could issue a withering comment to his look, her attention was distracted by the sound of someone running through the tall pasture grass.

It was Tadd, racing as fast as his short legs could carry him straight toward Judd. A breathless excitement glowed in his face, the mop of brown hair swept away from his forehead by the wind he generated with his running.

"Is that your horse?" The shrill pitch of his voice and his headlong flight toward the horse spooked the big gray. It plunged under Judd's rein, but its dancing hooves and big size didn't slow Tadd down. "Can I have a ride?"

"Tadd, look out!" Valerie shouted the warning as the gray horse reared and it looked as if Tadd was going to run right under those pawing hooves.

In the next second he was scooped off the ground and lifted into the saddle, Judd's arms around his waist. Her knees went weak with relief.

"Hasn't your mother taught you that you don't run up to a horse like that?" Judd reprimanded the boy he held, but Valerie noticed the glint of admiration in his look that

Tadd had not been afraid. "It scares a horse. You have to let them know you're near and walk up slowly."

"I'll remember," Tadd promised, but with a reckless smile that reminded Valerie of Judd. "Will you give me a ride? I've never been on a horse before."

"You're on one now," Judd pointed out. "What do you think of it?"

Tadd leaned to one side to peer at the ground, his eyes slightly rounded as he straightened. "It's kind of a long way down, isn't it?"

"You'll get used to it." Judd lifted his gaze from the dark-haired boy to glance at Valerie. "I'll give him a short ride around the pasture."

"You don't have to," she replied stiffly, and tried to figure out why she resented that Tadd was having his first ride with Judd, his father, and not her. "Worming your way into Tadd's favor won't get you anywhere with me."

A dangerous glint appeared in his look. "Until this moment that hadn't occurred to me. I have a whole flock of nieces and nephews who are always begging for rides, and I lumped your son into their category. I know you're disappointed that I can't admit to a more ulterior and devious motive."

Their exchange was sailing over Tadd's head. He couldn't follow it, but he had caught one of the things Judd had said. "Are you going to really give me a ride?" he asked.

"If your mother gives her permission," Judd told him in silent challenge to Valerie.

At the beseeching look from her son, she nodded her head curtly. "You have my permission."

"Thank you," Judd said mockingly as he reined the spirited gray away from the fence.

At a walk, they started across the grassy field. Tadd laughed and nearly bounced out of the saddle when the horse went into a trot, but he didn't sound or look the least bit frightened. After making a sweeping arc into the pasture, Judd turned the horse toward the fence and cantered him back to where Valerie was waiting.

With one hand, he swung Tadd to the ground. "Remember what I told you. From now on, you'll *walk* up to a horse." Tadd gave him a solemn nod of agreement. With a last impersonal glance at Valerie, Judd backed his mount away from the small boy before turning it toward its home stables.

"Come on, Tadd," Valerie called to him. "Let's go to the house and have something cold to drink."

He lingered for a minute in the pasture watching Judd ride away, a sight that pulled at Valerie, too, but she resisted it. Finally he ran toward her and Valerie wondered if he knew any other speed. He ducked under the fence as if he had been doing it all his life. He skipped along beside her, chattering endlessly about the ride.

"Where did you two disappear to?" Clara asked when Valerie reached the houseyard. Her question bordered on an accusation.

"I went for a ride," Tadd chimed out an answer, unaware he wasn't the second person Clara had meant.

"We just walked along the fence," Valerie answered, realizing a bushy shade tree had blocked her and Judd from Clara's sight.

"What was his business?" The tone was skeptical that there had been any such reason.

"He offered to buy the place," Valerie answered, and murmured to herself, "among other things!"

CHAPTER FIVE

After much discussion and debate, Valerie persuaded Clara that the three of them should spend the summer on her grandfather's farm. She refused to be intimidated by Judd's proximity as a neighbor. This was the only chance she would ever have to show her son what it had been like for her to grow up in this house. And perhaps it would be the only time she would have to devote solely to Tadd while he was in his formative years.

Eventually she swayed Clara into going along with her. Once the agreement had been reached, they had to tackle the problem of arranging things in Cincinnati to be absent for possibly three months.

Clara's married sister agreed to send both of them more clothes from the apartments, forward their mail, and see that everything was locked up. Valerie's telephoned request to her employer for an extended leave of absence received a notification of her dismissal, as Clara had warned. But all in all, the arrangements were made with minimal complications.

Amid all this was the decision of what to

107

do about the farm and consultation with Jefferson Burrows, the attorney. At the end of the following week Valerie came to the decision she had known all along she would have to make. After confiding in Clara, she sought out Mickey at the stables.

Valerie came straight to the point. "I wanted to let you know, Mick, that I've decided to sell the farm."

Sitting in the shade of the building, cleaning some leather tack, the retired jockey didn't even glance up when she made the announcement. He spat on the leather and polished some more.

"Then you'll be selling the horses?" he asked.

"Yes, I'll have to," she nodded.

"Since you're not keeping the place, you'll be better off to sell them soon," Mickey advised. "Were you going to have an auction?"

"Yes. Mr. Burrows, the lawyer, said if I decided to sell the horses, an auction could be scheduled within two weeks," she explained.

"It won't give you much time to do very much advertising," he shrugged, "but word has a way of getting around fast among horsemen. I'm sure you'll have a good turnout. As soon as you set the date, I'll call some of my friends in the business and start spreading the word."

"Thanks, Mick."

"It's the least I can do. There is one thing, though." He put the halter aside and stood up. "You see that bay mare grazing off by herself?"

Valerie glanced toward the paddock he faced and saw the bay mare he meant, a sleek, long-legged animal with a chestnut brown coat with black points.

"She's a beauty," Valerie commented in admiration.

"Don't put Ginger in the auction," Mickey said, and explained, "She's the best get out of old Donnybrook, but she's barren, no good for breeding at all. She's got no speed, but she's a good hack, might even make it as a show jumper. But you'd never get your money's worth out of her in a breeding sale. If I was you, I'd advertise her as a hunter and try to sell her that way."

"Thanks, I'll do that," she promised. His thoughtfulness and ready acceptance of her decision made her feel a little guilty. This farm and these horses were practically like his own. He had lived here and taken care of all the animals here, many of them since birth. Now they were being sold and he was out of a job and a place to live. "What will you do, Mickey? Where will you go?"

"Don't worry about me, Valerie," he laughed. "I've had a standing offer from Judd for years to come to work for him taking care of his young colts. He claims that I'm the best he's ever seen at handling the young ones."

The mention of Judd's name made her glance toward the paddock again to conceal her expression. "Judd wants to buy this," she said.

"Are you going to sell it to him?" he asked, not surprised by her statement.

"It depends on whether or not I get an offer better than the one he makes." Common sense made her insist that it didn't matter who ultimately purchased the property. She wouldn't be here when they took possession.

"If Judd has set his mind on buying it, he'll top any reasonable offer you get," Mickey grinned. " 'Cause once he makes up his mind he wants somethin', he seldom lets anything stand in his way till he gets it."

It was a statement that came echoing back a week later. Valerie was walking out of the bank in town just as Judd was coming in. Courtesy demanded that she speak to him, at least briefly.

"Hello, Judd." She nodded with forced

pleasantness, and would have walked on by him, but he stopped.

"Hello, Valerie. I saw the auction notice." His tone sounded only conversational.

"For the horses? Yes, in less than two weeks from now," she admitted. His gaze was inspecting her in a most bemused fashion. Valerie had the feeling a strap was showing or something, and her hand moved protectively to the elastic neckline of the peasant-styled knit top. "Is something wrong?" she queried a bit sharply.

"You look very cool and proper with your hair fixed like that," Judd answered. It was pulled away from her face into a loose chignon at the back of her head.

"It's a very warm day. I feel cooler if my hair is away from my neck," Valerie replied as if her change of hairstyle required an explanation.

"It's attractive, but it isn't exactly you," he commented in a knowing voice. Without skipping a beat, he continued, "I suppose once all the legal arrangements are completed after the auction you'll be leaving?"

"We're staying a little longer." She didn't see the need to tell him she would be there for the summer. He would discover it soon enough, so there was no point in informing him in advance.

"We?" A jet-dark brow lifted at the plural.

"Yes — Tadd, Clara and myself," Valerie admitted.

"The old battle-ax isn't leaving, either, huh?" But the way he spoke the word was oddly respectful. Then his manner became withdrawn. "I must be keeping you from your errands. Will you be at the auction?"

"Yes." She was a bit puzzled by his behavior and curious as to why he hadn't mentioned anything about buying her land.

"I'll probably see you there," he said.

Valerie had the feeling she was being brushed off. "Probably," she answered with a cool smile, her chin lifted stiffly, then walked away.

Between that brief meeting in town and the auction, she didn't see Judd. She ignored the knotting ache in her stomach and told herself she was glad she had finally convinced him that she wanted nothing to do with him. She was positive Judd had only pursued her at the beginning of her return because he had thought she would be easy. Now he knew differently. She wasn't easy and she wasn't available.

But the way her heart catapulted at the sight of his familiar figure in the auction crowd made a mockery of her silent disclaimers of interest in him. It was a bitter admission to recognize that she was still half in love with him.

The stable and house yard was littered with cars, trucks and horse trailers. There seemed to be an ocean of buyers, lookers and breeders. Around the makeshift auction ring was an encircling cluster of people jostling to get a look at the brood mare up for bids.

Valerie looked for Tadd and saw him firmly holding on to Mickey's hand, as if concerned he might get separated from his friend in the shuffle of people. Another look found Judd working his way through the crowd toward the trailer being used as the auctioneer's office.

A horse neighed behind her, a nervous sound that betrayed its agitation at the unusual commotion going on around it. Valerie turned to watch a groom walking the horse in a slow circle to calm it, crooning softly. All the horses looked sleek and in excellent condition, thanks to Mickey's unstinting efforts.

She glanced back to the auction ring where in a rhythmic droning voice the auctioneer was making his pitch. She walked in the opposite direction to the relative peace and quiet of the stables. Here the fever pitch of activity was reduced to a low hum as the grooms Mick had handpicked for the day prepared the brood mares and colts for the sale.

The warm air was pungent with the smell of horses. Straw rustled beneath shifting feet. Valerie wandered down the row of stalls, pausing to stroke the velvet nose thrust out toward her. She stopped at the paddock entrance to the barns and gazed out over empty pastures.

"It looks strange, doesn't it, not to see any mares grazing out there with their foals," Judd commented with an accurate piece of mind reading.

Valerie jumped at the sound of his voice directly behind her. "You startled me," she said in accusing explanation.

"Sorry," he offered, but she doubted that he meant it. "Is the auction going well?"

"So far," she answered with a shrug, and turned to look out the half door to the pasture. "It's bedlam out there," she said to explain her reason for escaping to the barns.

"A lot of buyers is what sends the prices up," Judd reminded her. "And, from the sound of the bidding on the number-fourteen mare, Misty's Delight, she's going to bring top dollar."

"Misty's Delight," Valerie repeated, and released a short, throaty laugh. "When I saw the names on the sale catalogue, I didn't know any of the horses. Granddad called that mare Misty's Delight by the name of Maude. As far as I'm concerned, they aren't selling Black Stockings. They're auctioning Rosie, or Sally or Polly."

"Yes, I'm glad your grandfather isn't here. Those mares were his pets, and the stallion, Donnybrook, was the most precious to him of them all," Judd admitted.

"If granddad were here, there wouldn't be a sale. There wouldn't be any need for one," Valerie sighed, and turned away from the empty paddocks. "But there is. And I'm selling. And I'm not going to have any regrets," she finished on a note of determination.

"Have you listed the farm for sale yet?" he asked, taking it for granted that she was selling it.

Since it was true, she didn't see any point in going into that side issue. "In a way," she answered, and explained that indecisive response. "It won't officially be listed for another couple of weeks."

"Why the delay?" He studied her curiously.

"I had a couple of appraisals from two local real estate agents," Valerie began.

"Yes, I know," Judd interrupted. "I saw

them, and I'm prepared to buy it for two thousand more than the highest price they gave you."

She took a deep breath at his handsome offer and nibbled at her lip, but didn't comment on his statement. "They suggested I'd be able to get about five thousand more if I painted all the buildings. So I'm going to take some of the profits from the horse sale and have everything painted."

"I'll match that, and you can forget about the painting," he countered. "I'd just have to do it all over again in the Meadow Farms' colors."

Leaning back against a wooden support post, Valerie eyed him warily, unable to trust him. She knew how vulnerable she was; she had only to check her racing pulse to be reminded of that. So she was doubly cautious about becoming involved in any dealings with him.

"Tell me the truth, Judd, why are you so determined to buy Worth Farms?" she demanded, her mouth thinning into a firm line.

A brow arched at her challenge as he tipped his head to one side, an indefinable glint in his eyes. "Why are you so determined to believe that I have some reason other than business?"

"Don't forget that I know you, Judd Prescott," she countered.

The corners of his mouth deepened. "You know me as intimately as any woman ever has, considerably more so than most." He taunted her with the memory of their affair.

Her cheeks flamed hotly as conflicting emotions churned inside of her. "I meant that I know you as a man."

"I should hope so," Judd drawled, deliberately misinterpreting her meaning.

"In the general sense," she corrected in anger.

"That's a pity." He rested a hand on the post she was leaning against, but didn't move closer. "Meadow Farms needs your grandfather's acreage, the pastures, the grass, the hay fields. The stables and barns can be used for the weanlings and the yearlings. The house can be living quarters for any of my married help who might need it. If the old battle-ax had inherited it, I would still want to buy it. Have you got that clear, Valerie?" His level gaze was serious.

"Yes," she nodded, a stiff gesture that held a hint of resentment.

"Good." Judd straightened, taking his hand from the post and offering it to her to seal their bargain. "Have we got a deal?"

"Yes." Wary, Valerie hesitated before placing her hand in his and added the qualification, "On purely a business level."

"Strictly business." He gripped her hand and let it go, a faint taunting smile on his lips. "The matter is in the hands of our respective attorneys. We've agreed on the price, so the only thing left is for me to pay you the money for your signature deeding the land to me."

"There's just one thing," Valerie added.

"Oh? What's that?" Judd asked with distant curiosity.

"I'm not giving you possession of the house until the first of September. The barns, the stables, the pastures, everything else you can have when we sign the papers, except the house," she told him.

"And why is that?" He seemed only mildly interested.

"Because that's how long we'll be staying. I want to have this summer with Tadd," Valerie explained with a trace of defensiveness. "With working and all, I haven't been able to spend much time with him up until now. He's been growing up with babysitters. I've decided to devote this summer to him and begin working again this fall when he goes back to school."

"In that case, the house is yours until the

first of September," Judd agreed with an indifferent shrug. "Are there any other conditions?"

"No." She shook her head, her long toffee hair swinging freely around her shoulders.

"Then everything is all settled," he concluded.

"I guess it is."

It all worked as smoothly as Judd had said it would. The matter was turned over to their attorneys. There wasn't even a need for Valerie to see Judd. When all the estate, mortgage and legal matters were completed, Jefferson Burrows brought out to the house the papers she needed to sign and gave her a check. The property became Judd's without any further communication between them and the documents gave her possession of the house until the first of September. It was all strictly business.

Something jumped on her bed, but the mattress didn't give much under its weight. "Mom? You'd better get up," Tadd insisted.

Valerie opened one sleepy eye to identify her son and rolled onto her stomach to bury her head under a pillow. "It's early. Go back to sleep, Tadd."

His small hand shook her bare shoulder in

determined persistence. "Mom, what's that man doing on a ladder outside your window?" he demanded to know.

"A ladder?" she repeated sleepily, and lifted her head from under the pillow to frown at the pajama-clad boy sitting on her bed. "What are you talking about, Tadd?"

His attention was riveted on her bedroom window. A scraping sound drew her bleary gaze, as well. The sleep was banished from her eyes at the sight of a strange man wearing paint-splattered white overalls standing on a ladder next to her window.

"What's he doing there, mom?" Tadd frowned at her.

There wasn't a shade at the window, nothing to prevent the man from looking in and seeing her. Valerie was angered by the embarrassing situation she was in. She tugged the end of the bedspread from the foot of the bed and pulled it with her. It was white chenille with a pink rose design woven in the center. She sat up on the side of her bed with her back to the window.

She picked up the alarm clock on the small table. Its hands pointed to seven o'clock. She began wrapping the bedspread around her sarong-fashion, fighting its length as her temper mounted. Pushing her sleep-rumpled hair away from one side of her face and tucking it behind her ear, she rose from the bed.

Tadd followed. "What's he doing there?" he repeated.

"That's what I'm about to find out!" she snapped, flinging a corner of the bedspread over her shoulder in a gesture unconsciously reminiscent of a caped crusader.

She stalked to the staircase and hitched the bedspread up around her ankles to negotiate the steps. Part of the white bedspread trailed behind her like a train and she had to keep yanking it along to prevent Tadd from tripping on it.

As she slammed out of the screen door onto the porch, another white-clad stranger was walking by carrying a stepladder. At the sight of Valerie, he stopped and stared.

"Would you mind telling me what's going on here?" she demanded, ignoring his incredulous and slightly ogling look. "And where are you going with that ladder?"

"Don't look at me, ma'am." The man backed away, absolving himself of any blame. "I just do what I'm told. The boss said I was to come here and I'm here."

"Where is your boss? I want to speak to him." Valerie forgot to hitch up the spread before starting down the porch steps and nearly tripped.

"He . . . he's on the other side of the house," the man stuttered as one side of the spread slipped, revealing the initial curving swell of one breast before Valerie tucked the material back in place.

She had taken one step in the direction the flustered man had indicated when she heard the cantering beat of horse's hooves and looked around to see Judd riding up on the big gray. She stopped and glanced back at the man.

"You can go on about your business now," she snapped.

"Yes, ma'am!" He scurried off as if he had been shot.

Tadd stood on the porch, one bare foot resting on top of the other. He was watching the proceedings with innocent interest, curious and wide-eyed. Like his mother, his attention had become focused on Judd, who was dismounting to walk to the house. Valerie stepped forward to confront him.

"Would you like to explain to me what these men are doing here at this hour of the morning?" she demanded, her nostrils distending slightly in temper.

"I came by to let you know I'd hired a contractor to paint the place. I think I'm a little late." As he spoke, his gaze was making a leisurely inspection from her tousled mane of honey-dark hair down her bedspread-wrapped length and returning for an overall view of her alluring dishabille.

At the touch of his green-eyed gaze on her bare shoulder and its lingering interest on the point where the white material jutted out to cover her breasts, Valerie tugged the spread more tightly around her. She realized he was very much aware that she was naked beneath it.

"A little late is an understatement," she fumed. "I woke up this morning to find a man outside my bedroom window on a ladder!"

"If I'd known you slept in the altogether, I would have been the man on the ladder outside your window," Judd drawled with soft suggestiveness.

An irritated sound of exasperation came from her throat. "It's impossible talking to you. I'll speak to the contractor myself and tell him to come back at a decent hour!" As she started to take a step, her leg became tangled in the folds of the bedspread.

Judd reached out with a steadying hand on her arm. "I think you'd better go back into the house before you trip and reveal more of your considerable charms than you'd like." He lifted her off her feet and into his arms before she could suspect his intention. The bedspread swaddled her into a cocoon that didn't lend itself to movement.

"Put me down!" Valerie raged in fiery embarrassment.

A lazy smile curved his mouth as he looked down at her. "I hired house painters, not nude artists. Not that I wouldn't object to having a private portrait of you."

She caught sight of Tadd staring at them with open-mouthed amazement. "Will you stop it?" she hissed at Judd, and he just chuckled, knowing she was at his mercy.

"Will you open the door for me, Tadd," he requested in an amused voice as he carried Valerie onto the porch.

Tadd scampered forward in his bare feet to comply, staring at Valerie's reddened face as Judd carried her past him. He followed them inside, letting the screen door close with a resounding bang. In the entry hall, Judd stopped.

"Now will you put me down?" Valerie demanded through clenched teeth, burning with mortification and a searing awareness of her predicament.

"Of course," he agreed with mocking compliance.

The arm at the back of her legs relaxed its hold, letting her feet slide to the floor while his other hand retained a light, steadying grip around her waist. Having both feet on the floor didn't give Valerie any feeling of advantage. Without shoes, the top of her head barely reached past his chin. To see his face, she had to tip her head back, a much too vulnerable position. She chose instead to glare upward through the sweep of her lashes.

"I think it would be wise if you put some clothes on," he suggested dryly as his gaze swung downward from her face, "or at least rearrange your sarong, so that pink rose adorns a less eye-catching spot."

His finger traced the outline of a rosebud design on the chenille bedspread. In doing so, he drew a circle around the hard button of her breast. Heat raced over her skin as Valerie jerked the bedspread higher, pulling the rose design almost to her collarbone. Judd chuckled for the second time, knowing how deeply he had disturbed her.

Spinning away from him, Valerie lifted the folds of the material up around her knees and bolted for the staircase. On the second step she stopped, remembering the predicament that awaited her upstairs. She sent an angry look over her shoulder.

"You go out there and tell that painter to get away from my window!" she ordered in an emotion-choked voice.

"I'll have him on the ground at once." Judd grinned at her, laughter dancing wickedly in his eyes.

Valerie glanced at the boy standing beside him. "Tadd, you come with me," she commanded. "It's time you were dressed, too."

Reluctantly Tadd moved toward the stairs. As Judd started toward the door, Valerie began climbing the steps to the second floor. Clara met her at the head of the stairs, her nightgown ruffling out from beneath the hem of her quilted robe.

"What's all the commotion about?" Clara ran a frowning look over Valerie's attire. "And what are you doing dressed like that?"

"Mr. Prescott neglected to inform us that he'd hired some painters to come out to the farm," was the short-tempered reply. "I woke up to find one outside my window on a ladder." Bunching the spread more tightly around her hips, Valerie started toward her bedroom.

"I've told you about going to bed like that," Clara's reproving voice followed her. "Haven't I warned you that someday there'd be a fire or something and you'd be caught!"

Valerie stopped abruptly to make a sharp retort and Tadd, who was following close behind her, bumped into her. Her hand gripped his shoulder to steady him and remained there as she sent Clara a look that would have withered the leaves from a mighty oak, but Clara was made of stronger stuff.

Swallowing the remark she had intended to make, Valerie muttered, "You're a lot of comfort, Clara," and glanced at the small boy. "Come on, Tadd. Let's get you dressed first."

Altering her course, she pushed Tadd ahead of her to her old bedroom that Tadd now occupied. While she went to the dresser to get his clean clothes, Tadd padded to the window and peered out.

"I don't see those men anymore, mommy. Judd made them go away," he told her.

"Good. Now off with those pajamas and into these clothes," she ordered curtly.

When Tadd was dressed, Valerie sent him downstairs and went to her own room. She made certain there wasn't a painter anywhere near the vicinity of her window before getting dressed herself. When she came downstairs she walked to the kitchen where the aroma of fresh-perked coffee wafted invitingly in the air.

Tadd was sitting at the breakfast table. An elbow was resting on the top and a small hand supported his forehead, pushing his brown hair on end. A petulant scowl marked his expression.

"Mom, Clara says I have to drink some of my milk before I have another pancake." He glared at the stout woman standing at the stove. "Do I have to? Can't I drink it afterward, mom? Please?"

Valerie glanced at the glass of white liquid that hadn't been touched. "Drink your milk, Tadd."

"Aw, mom!" he grumbled, and reached for the glass.

"Don't fix any pancakes for me, Clara." Ignoring her son, Valerie walked to the cupboard and poured a cup of coffee. "I'm not hungry."

"You'd better eat something," the woman insisted.

Before Valerie could argue the point, there was a knock on the back door and a taunting voice asked, "Are you decent in there?"

"Yes!" Valerie shot the sharply affirmative retort at the wire mesh where Judd's dark figure was outlined, and carried her cup to the table.

The hinges creaked as the screen door opened and Judd walked in. "The coffee smells good," he remarked. After one dancing took at Valerie's still simmering expression, he addressed his next words to Clara. "Do you mind if I have a cup?"

"Help yourself," the woman agreed with an indifferent shrug.

As he walked to the counter on which the coffeepot sat, Valerie watched the easy way he moved. His broad shoulders and chest, his narrow male hips, and the muscled columns of his long legs moved in perfect harmony. His body was programmed and conditioned to perform every task well. An ache quivered through her as Valerie remembered how well.

Pausing at the stove, Judd observed, "Pancakes for breakfast. Buckwheat?"

"Yes." Clara expertly flipped one from the griddle.

"Help yourself, Judd," Valerie heard herself offering in a caustic tone born out of a sense of inevitability. In an agitated desire for movement she rose from her chair to add more coffee to her steaming cup. "Orange juice. Bacon. Toast." She listed the choices. "Just help yourself to anything."

"Anything?" The soft, lilting word crossed the room to taunt her. She pivoted and caught her breath as his gaze leisurely roamed over her shape to let her know his choice.

She felt as if her toes were curling from the heat spreading through her. She turned away from his disturbing look and breathed an emotionally charged, "You know very well what I meant." Adding a drop more coffee to her cup, Valerie silently acknowledged that she didn't have many defenses against him left, certainly none when the topic became intimate. She attempted to change it. "Did you straighten those painters out about starting work at such an hour?" she demanded.

"In a manner of speaking," Judd replied, casually accepting the change in subject matter. "They started early to avoid working in the heat of the day. Unfortunately, they were under the impression that all the buildings were vacant, including the house. They know better now," he added with faint suggestiveness.

Valerie didn't need to be reminded of the early-morning episode. The absence of a direct answer to her first question prompted her to ask, "You did arrange for them to begin work at a more respectable hour, didn't you?"

"No," he denied. "There isn't any reason to change their working hours —"

"No reason?" she began indignantly.

But Judd continued, "However, from

now on they'll be working on the barns and stables in the mornings."

"I should hope so," Valerie retorted tightly.

"I drank some of my milk," Tadd piped up, a white moustache above his upper lip. "Can I have another pancake now?" Clara set another one in front of him. As Tadd reached for the syrup, he glanced at Judd. "They're very good. Do you want one?"

"No, thank you. I've already had my breakfast." Judd drained the last of the coffee from his cup. "It's time I was leaving. If the painters give you any trouble, Valerie, call me."

"I will," she agreed, but she could have told him that the only one who gave her trouble was himself. He troubled her mentally and emotionally, and there didn't seem to be any relief in sight.

CHAPTER SIX

A restlessness raced through Valerie. She tried to contain it as she had for the last several days, but it wouldn't be suppressed. There had been too much time on her hands lately, she reasoned. She was accustomed to working eight hours, coming home and working eight hours more with meals, housework and wash. But here the workload of the house was shared with Clara and she had no job except to play with Tadd.

One of the painters had a radio blaring a raucous brand of music that scraped at her nerves. Of the half a dozen men painting the barns and stables, there always seemed to be one walking around, getting paint, moving ladders, doing something, which was more than Valerie could say for herself.

Sighing, she left the porch and entered the house. Clara was in the living room, watching her favorite soap opera on television. Her gaze was glued to the screen and she didn't even glance up when Valerie entered the room.

"Clara," Valerie began, only to be silenced by an upraised hand. A couple of minutes later a commercial came on and she was allowed to finish what she had started to say. "I'm going to take Ginger out for a ride. Tadd is upstairs having a nap. Will you keep an eye on him while I'm gone?"

"Sure. Go ahead," her friend agreed readily.

Outside, Valerie dodged the gauntlet of ladders and paint cans to retrieve the bridle and saddle from the tack room. Several people had been out to look at the bay mare Mickey Flanners had suggested she sell privately, but so far no one had bought her. Valerie didn't mind. One horse wasn't that difficult to take care of and Tadd enjoyed the rides she took him on.

The bay mare trotted eagerly to the pasture fence when she approached. Lonely without her former equine companionship, the mare readily sought human company. There was never any difficulty catching her and she accepted the bit between her teeth as if it were sugar.

Astride the animal, Valerie turned the brown head toward the rolling land of the empty pasture. The mare stepped out quickly, moving into a brisk canter at a slight touch from Valerie's heel. She had no destination in mind. Her only intention was to try to run off this restlessness that plagued her.

The long-legged thoroughbred mare seemed prepared to run forever, clearing pasture fences like the born jumper Mickey had claimed she was. Valerie rode without concentrating on anything but the rhythmic stride of the animal beneath her and the pointed ears of its bobbing head.

When the bay horse slowed to a walk, Valerie wasn't aware that it was responding to her pressure on the reins. They entered a stand of trees and she ducked her head to avoid a low-hanging branch. When she straightened, it was in a clearing. Her fingers tightened on the reins, stopping the bay, as the blood drained from her face.

Unconsciously she had guided the mare to the place where she and Judd had met. From a long-ago habit, she dismounted and wound the reins around the broken branch of a tree. The mare lowered her head, blew at the grass and began to graze.

Almost in a trance, Valerie looked around her. The place hadn't seemed to change very much. The grass looked taller and thicker, promising a softer bed. She tore her gaze from it and noticed that lightning had taken a large limb from the oak tree some time ago.

Wrapping her arms tightly around her stomach, she tried to assuage the hollow ache. There was a longing for Judd so intense that it seemed to eat away at her insides. She wanted to cry from the joy she had once known here and the heartache that had followed, but no tears came.

It was crazy — it was foolish — it was destroying to want him. She was so successful at stimulating his lusty appetite, why hadn't she ever been able to arouse his love, she wondered. She was so filled with love that she thought she would explode.

The bay mare lifted her head, her ears pricking. Her sides heaved with a long, questioning whicker. Then the soft swish of grass behind her made Valerie turn as a big gray horse stopped at the edge of the clearing and Judd dismounted. He walked toward her with smooth, unhurried strides like a page from the past. Her heart lodged somewhere in the vicinity of her throat. She was unable to speak, half-afraid that she might discover she was dreaming.

But his voice was no dream: "I knew you'd come here sooner or later." Neither was the smoldering light in his green eyes as he came closer.

The instant he touched her, Valerie was convinced it wasn't a dream and she knew she didn't dare stay. "It was an accident," she insisted, her breath quickening. "I didn't mean to come here."

She tried to push out of his arms and make her way past him, but a sinewed arm hooked her waist and pulled her against his side. A muscled thigh brushed her legs apart to rub against her, while the hand at the small of her back pressed her close to him. His fingers cupped the side of her face and lifted it for inspection.

"Ever since the day you returned, I knew you would eventually come here." His gaze roamed possessively over her features. "You can't fight it any more than I can. It's always been that way with us."

"Yes." Her whispered agreement carried the throb of admission.

As his mouth descended on hers, Valerie realized his persistence had finally eroded her resolve. The surroundings, her love, the feel of him were more than she could withstand and she surrendered to the pulsing fire of his embrace.

Her lips parted under the insistence of his. His practiced hands molded her more fully against his length, but this closeness only heightened their mutual dissatisfaction with their upright position.

Burying his face in the curve of her neck, Judd swept her into his arms and carried her the few feet to the grassy nest. Kneeling, he laid her upon it, lifting the heavy mass of tawny hair and fanning it above her head. Her hands were around his neck to pull him down beside her, part of his weight crushing her.

"I've waited a long time to see that honey cloud of hair on that green pillow." His husky voice vibrated with passion. "And to see that love-drugged look in your cat eyes."

His mouth kissed the hollow of her throat as his skilled fingers unbuttoned her blouse. His hand wandered over the bareness of her waist and taut stomach. Its leisurely pace sent a languorous feeling floating through her limbs. His mouth trailed a fiery path to intimately explore the rounded softness of her breast. Her nails dug into the rippling muscles of his back and Judd brought his hard lips back to hers. More of his weight moved onto her.

He rubbed his mouth against the outline of her lips. "There were times when I wondered whether I had the control or the patience to wait for you to come here," he admitted. "I knew you'd been hurt and used badly. But I was also positive that I could make you forget the man who got you pregnant and ran off."

"Forget?" Her breathless laugh was painful and bitter, because he had made her forget. With a twist, she rolled from beneath him and staggered to her feet, shakily buttoning her blouse. "How could I forget?" The questioning statement was issued to herself. "You are that man, Judd."

Stunned silence greeted her tautly spoken announcement. Then Valerie heard him rise and a steel claw hooked her elbow to spin her around. A pair of blazing green eyes burned into her face.

"What are you saying?" Judd ground out savagely.

"You're Tadd's father," she informed him with flashing defiance. "I was almost three months pregnant when I left here seven years ago. Granddad threw me out because I wouldn't tell him who the father was. It was you . . . you and your damned virility!"

"If it's true, why didn't you come to me seven years ago and tell me you were pregnant?" Judd demanded.

"If it's true?" Valerie repeated with a taunting laugh. "You just answered your own question, Judd. You're the one and only man who has ever made love to me. But to you, I was just a cheap little tramp."

"That isn't true," he denied.

"Isn't it?" she mocked. "Why should I have endured the humiliation of telling you and have you question whether you were responsible?"

"I would have helped you," Judd replied grimly.

"What would you have done?" Valerie challenged. "Given me money for an abortion? Or paid me hush money to keep quiet about your part in it? You made me feel small enough without taking money from you."

"I never guessed you felt that way." A muscle in his jaw was flexing.

"I don't think you ever considered the possibility that I had feelings," she retorted. "I'm a human being with feelings and a heart, Judd. I'm not made of stone like you. Look — I even bleed." She scratched her nails across the inside of her arm, tiny drops of red appearing in the welts.

He caught at the hand that had marked her. "You crazy little fool!" he growled, and yanked her into his arms, crushing her tightly against him, the point of his chin rubbing the top of her head.

For an instant Valerie let herself enjoy the hard comfort of his arms before she rebelled. "Let me go, Judd." She strained against his hold. "Haven't you done enough?"

He partially released her, keeping one

arm firmly around her shoulders as he drew her along with him. "Come on."

"No!" She didn't know where he was taking her.

Stopping in front of the bay mare, Judd lifted her into the saddle. "I'm taking you back," he said, and handed her the reins.

"I can find my own way," she retorted. "I always did before."

His hand held the mare's bridle, preventing Valerie from reining her away. "This time I'm going with you," he stated.

"Why?" Valerie watched him with a wary eye when he walked to the big gray.

Judd didn't respond until he had mounted and ridden the high-stepping gray over beside her. "I'd like to have another look at my son."

Her fingers tightened on the reins and the mare tossed her head in protest. "Tadd is mine. You merely fathered him. He's mine, Judd," she warned.

He didn't argue the point and instead gestured for her to lead the way to her grandfather's farm, one that Judd now owned. They cantered in silence, their horses skittish and nervous, picking up the tenseness of their riders.

Tadd had awakened from his nap when they arrived. He didn't rush out to greet

Valerie, but remained sitting on the porch step, sulking because she had gone riding without him. Valerie was nervous as she walked to the house with Judd. Tadd was no longer just another little boy to him. He was his son, and Judd's green eyes were studying, inspecting and appraising the small boy.

"Did you have a good nap, Tadd?" Valerie asked with forced brightness.

"Why didn't you wait until I was up and take me for a ride?" he pouted.

"Because I wanted to go by myself," she answered, and promised, "You and I can go later this afternoon."

"Okay," Tadd sighed, accepting the alternative, and glanced at Judd. "Hello. How come you were riding if Mom wanted to be by herself?"

"We happened to meet each other while I was on my way here," Judd explained easily, his attention not wavering from Tadd's face.

"Were you coming over here to tell those men to go away?" Tadd wondered. "There hasn't been any man outside Mommy's window since that other day. But one of them gave me a brush — I'll show you." In a flash, he was on his feet and darting to the far end of the porch.

Judd slid a brief glance in Valerie's direction. "Have you told him anything about . . . his father?" he asked quietly.

"No." She shook her head.

But his voice hadn't been pitched so softly that Tadd hadn't picked up a piece of the conversation. He came back, holding up a worn-out brush that had not been used in some time. The bristles were stiff and broken.

As he showed it to Judd, he glanced up. "I don't have a father. Do you?"

Judd's dark head lifted in faint surprise. Valerie couldn't tell whether it was from Tadd's directness or the acuteness of his hearing. Bemusement softened the corners of the hard male mouth.

"Yes, I had one, but he died a long time ago," Judd admitted, and tipped his head to one side to study Tadd more closely as he asked, "Did your father die?"

"No. I don't have a father," Tadd repeated with childlike patience. "Some kids don't, you know," he informed Judd with blinking innocence. "Three of the kids I go to school with don't have dads. Of course, Cindy Tomkins has two." He lost interest in that subject. "It's a pretty neat brush, isn't it?"

"It sure is," Judd agreed.

"I wanted to help them paint, but they said I couldn't. They said I was too little." Tadd's mouth twisted, his expression indicating it was a statement he had heard many times before. "I'll be seven on my next birthday. That isn't too little, is it?"

"I think you have to be ten years old before you can be a painter," Judd told him.

Valerie's nerves were wearing thin. There wasn't much more of this conversation she could tolerate. Judd had seen Tadd again and talked to him. Surely that was enough?

"Tadd, why don't you run into the house and see if there's a carrot in the refrigerator for Ginger. I think she'd like one," she suggested.

"Okay." He started to turn and stopped. "Can I feed it to her?"

"Of course," she nodded, and he was off, slamming the screen door and tearing through the house to the kitchen. Feeling the scrutiny of Judd's eyes, her gaze slid from his direction.

"He isn't too familiar with the birds and the bees, is he?" Judd commented dryly. "Some children don't have a father," he repeated Tadd's statement. "Is that what you told him?"

"No, it's a conclusion he's reached all on his own. He has a general idea about the

143

birds and the bees, but he hasn't comprehended the significance of it," Valerie admitted, a shade defensively.

"What are you going to do when he does?" His level gaze never wavered from her. "What will you tell him when he asks about his father?"

"When he's old enough to ask the question, he'll be old enough to understand the truth," she retorted, knowing it was a day she didn't look forward to.

The sound of racing feet approached the porch in advance of the screen door banging open. "I got the carrot!" Tadd held it up. "Can I give it to Ginger now?"

At the nod from Valerie, Tadd started down the porch steps. As he went past Judd, he was cautioned, "Remember, Tadd, walk up to the horse."

With a carefree, "I will!" Tadd raced full speed halfway across the yard, then stopped to walk the rest of the way to the pasture fence where the bay mare was tied. Valerie watched him slowly feed the gentle mare.

"I feel that I owe you something for these last seven years," Judd said.

"You don't owe me anything." She shrugged away the suggestion, the idea stinging.

"I mean it, Valerie. I want to take care of

you and Tadd," he stated in a firm tone.

The full fury of her sparkling eyes was directed at him. "I wouldn't take your money then, Judd, and I won't take it now."

Instead of being angry, Judd looked amused by her fiery display. His gaze ran over her upturned face, alight with temper and pride.

"Tigress," he murmured. "All this doesn't change anything."

Unable to hold that look, Valerie glanced away. She seemed incapable of resisting him, but she tried anyway. "Yes, it does."

"Valerie." His voice commanded her attention. When she didn't obey, his fingers caught her chin and turned her to face him. "It isn't any use fighting it."

"I've made up my mind, Judd," she insisted stiffly. "I won't be your lover. Please! Just leave me alone."

His mouth slanted in amusement. "Do you think I haven't tried?" he mocked, and kissed her hard. When he straightened, he murmured, "And tell that battle-ax that it's impolite to eavesdrop." With that, he turned and walked across the yard to where the gray hunter was standing next to Valerie's mare.

The screen door opened and Clara stepped out. "Humph!" she snorted. "So it's impolite to eavesdrop, is it? What do you suppose they call what he was proposing?"

"You shouldn't have been listening," Valerie said, and continued to watch Judd, who had stopped to say goodbye to Tadd.

"You shouldn't carry on private conversations where people can overhear," Clara retorted. "So you decided to tell him he was the boy's father, did you?"

"Yes," Valerie admitted.

"What do you suppose he's going to do about it?"

"There isn't anything he can do. Tadd is mine. Judd knows that," Valerie insisted.

"Mark my words, he'll figure out a way to use it to his advantage. Judd Prescott is a tenacious man." There was a hint of admiration in Clara's voice as they both watched him ride away.

CHAPTER SEVEN

Judd came over twice more that week, ostensibly to check on the progress of the painting crew, but that possessive light was in his eyes whenever his gaze met Valerie's. It held a warning or a promise, depending on her mood at the time. His attitude toward Tadd remained relatively casual, a little more interested and occasionally warmer at different moments.

Valerie was in the kitchen helping Clara wash the breakfast dishes when a car drove into the yard. The painting crew had finished the day before, so she knew it wasn't one of them. As she walked to the front door, she wiped her hands dry on the towel and wondered if the lawyer, Jefferson Burrows, had more papers for her to sign.

Judd's visits had always been made on horseback. It didn't occur to her that the car might be driven by him. Not until she saw him step out. Tadd was outside playing and immediately stopped what he was doing to rush forward to greet Judd.

After sending one green-eyed glance toward Valerie standing on the porch, Judd directed his attention to the boy skipping along beside him. His hair gleamed jet black in the sunlight, with Tadd's a lighter hue.

"Do you have anything planned to do today?" Judd asked him.

"Mom and me are going riding later on," Tadd answered after thinking for a minute.

"That's something you could do tomorrow if you have a place to visit today, isn't it?" Judd suggested, and Valerie felt a tiny leap of alarm.

"I guess so," Tadd agreed, then frowned. "But we don't have a place to visit." The frown lifted. "How come you drove a car? Are you going to take us someplace?"

"I might," was the smiling response.

"Tadd, come into the house and wash your hands!" Valerie called sharply.

With a gleeful expression, Tadd came bounding to the porch hopping excitedly from one foot to the other. "Mom, did you hear? Judd said he might take us someplace."

"Yes, I heard what he said." She sent Judd an angry look and attempted to smile at her son. "Go into the house and wash your hands as you were told."

"Find out where we're going!" Tadd called over his shoulder, and hurried into the house.

Descending the porch steps, Valerie walked out to confront Judd. "Why did you tell Tadd we might be going someplace with you?" she demanded angrily. "It isn't fair to raise a little boy's hopes up like that."

"Why?" He returned her took with feigned innocence. "I came over to ask you and Tadd to spend the day with me. There's a tobacco auction over by Lothian, probably one of the last of the season. I thought Tadd might find it interesting."

"I'm sure he would find it very interesting, but we aren't going," she stated flatly. "And you shouldn't have let Tadd think we would."

"How did I know you'd refuse?" He smiled lazily. "I hadn't even asked you yet when I mentioned it to him."

"You knew very well I'd refuse!" she snapped.

"Temper, temper, little spitfire," Judd taunted.

"Of course I'm angry," Valerie argued defensively. "You've made me the villain as far as Tadd is concerned."

"You could always change your mind and agree to come with me," he reminded her.

"You know I won't."

"Yes, you will." His level gaze became deadly serious. "Otherwise I'll have to have a talk with Tadd and tell him who his father is."

Valerie paled. "You wouldn't do that!" she protested. "He wouldn't understand. He'd be hurt and confused. You wouldn't be that ruthless!"

"I'll have my way, Valerie." It wasn't an idle warning. "Will you come or shall I have a talk with Tadd?"

Tears burned the back of her eyes and she bit the inside of her lip to keep it from quivering. She had known he was hard, and not above using people to get what he wanted, and he'd already made it plain that he wanted her.

"If I agree to come, will you give me your word to say nothing to Tadd about being his father?" she demanded tightly.

"You have my word," Judd agreed, "if you come."

"I . . . I'll need a few minutes to change my clothes," Valerie requested.

His skimming gaze conveyed the message that he preferred her without any, but he said, "Take all the time you need. I'll be waiting."

Frustrated, Valerie ground out, "You can wait until hell freezes over and it still won't do any good!" Pivoting on her heel, she rushed into the house.

Fifteen minutes later she emerged cool and composed in a yellow-flowered cotton sun dress. Tadd's face and hands had been scrubbed and inspected by Clara, his shirt and pants changed to a clean set. Valerie couldn't help thinking that the three of them probably looked like the ideal American family, leaving on a day's outing to a tobacco auction in Lothian, Maryland. It hurt to know that they would never be a family in the legal sense, but Tadd's steady stream of chatter didn't give Valerie any time to dwell on that.

The sights, sounds and smells of the tobacco auction proved to be as fascinating to Valerie as they were to Tadd. Various grades of Maryland tobacco were sold off in lots. The rhythmic cadence of the auctioneer's voice rang through the area, the slurring words punctuated by a clear "Sold!" at the end. The summer air was aromatically pungent with the smell of stacks of drying tobacco leaves. Colors varied from dark gold to brown.

They wandered around the auction area and strolled through the warehouse. Tadd saw most of the scene from Judd's shoulders. They had a cold drink beneath a shade tree.

Later, Judd drove to a park and they picnicked from a basket his mother had packed. Through it all, Judd was at his charming best and Valerie found herself succumbing to his spell as if she didn't have better sense.

She took his hand, accepted the arm that occasionally encircled her shoulders, smiled into the green eyes that glinted at her, and warmed under the feather kisses Judd would bestow on the inside of her wrist or her hair. In spite of her better judgment, she relaxed and enjoyed his company, flirting with him and feeling carelessly happy all the while.

As they lingered at the picnic area, Judd peeled an orange and began feeding her sections while Tadd played on the swings. Each time a bead of juice formed on her lips he kissed it away until Tadd demanded his share of the attention by handing Judd an orange to peel for him.

When they started back in the early afternoon, Valerie was too content to care that it would soon be over. She closed her eyes and listened to the mostly one-sided conversation between Tadd and Judd. A faint smile tugged at the corners of her mouth from Tadd's domination.

The miles sped away beneath the swiftly turning tires. Valerie guessed that they were almost home, but she didn't want to open her eyes to see how close they were. A large male hand took hold of one of hers. Her lashes slowly lifted to watch Judd carry it to his mouth, kissing the sensitive palm. His gaze left the road in front of him long enough to send one lazy, sweeping glance at her.

"Did you enjoy yourself today?" he asked softly.

"Yes, very much," she admitted.

Tadd, who couldn't be silent for long, cried, "Look at all the horses, mommy!"

Dragging her gaze from Judd's compelling profile, she glanced out of the window. The familiar black fences of Meadow Farms were on either side of the car. She sat up straighter, realizing Judd had turned off the road that would have taken them to her grandfather's farm.

"Where are we going?" she asked. There was only one destination possible at the end of this lane: the headquarters of Meadow Farms.

"Are we going to see the horses?" Tadd asked, leaning over the seat.

"There's someone who wants to see you," Judd answered, glancing in Tadd's direction.

"See me?" His voice almost squeaked in disbelief. "Who?"

"Who?" Valerie echoed the demand, a quiver of uncertainty racing through her.

"Mickey Flanners," Judd answered. "When I mentioned I'd be seeing you today, he asked me to bring you over if we had time."

"I haven't seen Mickey in a long time," Tadd declared in a tone that exaggerated the time span.

"That's what he said." Judd slowed the car as the lane split ahead of them.

In one direction were the stables and barns of the thoroughbred breeding farm; in the other direction was the main house in which the Prescotts lived. Judd made the turn in the latter direction. Valerie, who had relaxed upon learning it was Mickey Flanners they were going to see, felt her nerves stretching tense.

The lane curled into a circular driveway in front of a large pillared house, glistening white in the bright afternoon sunlight. To Valerie, it appeared the embodiment of gracious living, a sharp contrast to the simple farmhouse in which she was raised.

"Is *this* where Mickey lives?" Tadd asked in an awed voice.

"No, this is where I live," Judd explained, stopping the car in front of the main entrance to the house. He glanced at Valerie

154

and saw the hesitation in her gold-flecked eyes. "I'll be on my mother's black list if I don't stop at the house first so she can say hello to you and Tadd."

"Judd, really. . . ." Valerie started to protest, but it was too late.

The front door of the house had opened and Judd's mother was coming out to greet them, petite and striking with those angel wings of silver in her dark hair. The white pleated skirt and the blue and white polka-dot top with a matching short-sleeved jacket in blue that Maureen Prescott wore was so casually elegant that Valerie felt self-conscious about her becoming but simple cotton sun dress.

"Here's mother now." Judd opened his door and stepped out.

It wasn't manners that kept Valerie inside the car. The magnificent house, the beautifully landscaped grounds, the status attached to the Prescott name, and the woman waiting on the portico warned her that she was out of her league.

Her door was opened and Judd stood waiting, a hand extended to help her out of the car. She turned her troubled and uncertain gaze to him. He seemed to study it with a trace of amusement that didn't make her feel any more comfortable.

"What happened to my tigress?" he chided softly. "You look like a shy little kitten. Come on." He reached in and took her hand to draw her out of the car.

Once she was standing beside him, Judd retained his hold of her hand. Valerie absorbed strength from his touch, but the twinges of unease didn't completely go away. It seemed a very long way from the car up the walk to the steps leading to the columned portico. To cover her nervousness, Valerie held herself more stiffly erect, her chin lifted a fraction of an inch higher than normal, her almond gold eyes wide and proud.

Tadd didn't appear to suffer from any of Valerie's pangs of self-consciousness. He skipped and hopped, turned and looked, and generally let his curious eyes take in everything there was to see. He exhibited no shyness at all when the unknown woman walked forward to meet them.

"Hello, Valerie. I'm so glad you were able to stop in," Judd's mother greeted her warmly, a smile of welcome curving her mouth.

"Thank you, Mrs. Prescott," Valerie answered, and suddenly wished that Judd would let go of her hand, but he didn't.

"Please, call me Maureen," the other

woman insisted with such friendliness that Valerie was reminded her reputation as hostess was without equal.

This open acceptance of her only made Valerie more uneasy. "That's very kind of you . . . Maureen." She faltered stiffly over the name.

Maureen Prescott either didn't notice or overlooked Valerie's stilted tones as she turned to Tadd, bending slightly at the waist. "And you must be Tadd."

After an admitting bob of his head, he asked, "How did you know me?"

The woman's smile widened. "I've heard a lot about you."

"Who are you?" Tadd wanted to know.

"I'm . . . Judd's mother."

Did Valerie imagine it or had there been a pulse beat of hesitation before Maureen Prescott had explained her relationship? Then Valerie realized she was being ridiculously oversensitive to the situation.

"Say hello to Mrs. Prescott, Tadd," Valerie prompted her son.

Dutifully he extended a hand to the woman facing him and recited politely, "Hello, Mrs. Prescott."

"Mrs. Prescott is quite a mouthful, isn't it?" The teasing smile on Maureen's lips was warm with understanding. "Why don't you call me Reeny, Tadd?" she suggested.

"Reeny is what my nieces and nephews call her," Judd explained quietly to Valerie. "When they were little, they couldn't pronounce her given name so they shortened it."

Valerie was uncomfortably aware that Tadd had been given permission to use the same name that the other grandchildren called their grandmother. She felt the creeping warmth of embarrassment in her cheeks. Did Maureen Prescott know Tadd was her grandchild? Had Judd told her?

Almost in panic, she searched the woman's face for any indication of hidden knowledge. But the turquoise eyes were clear without a trace of cognition. A tremor of relief quaked through Valerie. She wasn't sure she could have handled the situation if this genteel woman had known the truth.

"Reeny is nice," Tadd agreed to the name.

"I'm glad you like it, Tadd." Maureen Prescott straightened and cast an apologetic smile at Judd. "Frank Andrews called and left a message for you to phone him the instant you came back." With a glance at Valerie, she added, "It seems every time a person tries to set aside a day strictly for pleasure, something urgent like this crops up."

Valerie's head moved in a rigid nod of understanding before a slight movement from Judd drew her attention. A grim resignation had thinned his mouth and added a glitter of impatience in his eyes.

"I'm sorry, Valerie," he said in apology for the intrusion of business. "But it'll only take a few minutes to phone him."

"That's all right. Go ahead," she insisted, and untangled her fingers from the grip of his to clasp her hands nervously in front of her.

"While Judd is making his phone call, you and Tadd can come with me. After that long drive, I'm sure you're thirsty and I have a big pitcher of lemonade all made, as well as some cookies," Judd's mother invited.

"No, thank you, Mrs. Prescott . . . Maureen," Valerie refused quickly, and reached for Tadd's hand. "It's very kind of you, but Tadd and I will walk down to the stables and find Mickey."

"You'll do no such thing, Valerie." Judd's low voice rumbled through the air with ominous softness. Her sideways glance saw the hardened jaw and angry fire in his eyes. His look held a silent warning not to persist in her refusal of the invitation. "I'll be through in a few minutes to take you myself. In the meantime, I'm sure Tadd —" his gaze flicked to the boy "— would like to have some cookies and lemonade. Wouldn't you, Tadd?"

"Yes." The response was quick and without hesitation, followed by an uncertain glance at Valerie. "Please," Tadd added.

"Very well," Valerie agreed, smiling stiffly, and added a defensive, "If you are sure we aren't putting you to any trouble?"

"None at all," Judd's mother assured her, and turned to walk toward the front door.

Judd's fingers dug into the flesh of Valerie's arm in a punishing grip as he escorted her up the steps to the portico. At the wide double entrance to the house, he let her go to open the door for his mother, then waited for her and Tadd to precede him inside.

"Excuse me." Almost immediately upon entering, Judd took his leave from them. "I won't be long." His look warned Valerie that he expected to find her in the house when he was finished.

"We'll be on the veranda, Judd," his mother told him.

Valerie watched him walk away, skittishly becoming conscious of the expansive foyer dominated by a grand staircase rising to the second floor. The foyer was actually an enormously wide hallway splitting the house down the center with rooms branching off from it.

Furniture gleamed with the rich-grained luster of hardwood, adorned on top with vases of flowers and art objects. Valerie took a tighter grip on Tadd's hand, knowing she couldn't afford to replace anything he might accidentally break. It was a stunning, artfully decorated home, elegance and beauty blended to comfort, like something out of the pages of a magazine.

"We'll go this way." Maureen Prescott started forward to lead the way, the clicking sound of her heels on the white-tiled floor echoing through the massive house.

"You have a lovely home." Valerie felt obliged to make some comment, but her tone made the compliment sound uncertain.

"It's a bit intimidating, isn't it?" the woman laughed in gentle understanding. "I remember the first time Blane, Judd's father, brought me here to meet his parents. It was shortly after we'd become engaged, and the place terrified me. It was much more formal then. When Blane told me that we would live here after we were married, I wanted to break the engagement, but fortunately he talked me out of that."

Maureen Prescott's instinctive knowledge of Valerie's reaction allowed her to relax a little. It was comforting to know that someone else had been awed by this impressive home.

"The house is at its best when it's filled with people, especially children," Maureen continued in an affectionate voice. "It seems to come to life then. When my five were growing up, the house never seemed big enough — which sounds hard to believe, doesn't it?"

"A little," Valerie admitted.

"They seemed to fill every corner of it with their projects and pets and friends. That reminds me —" she glanced down at the brown-haired boy trotting along beside Valerie "— there's something outside that I want to show you."

"What is it?" Tadd asked, his olive brown eyes rounding.

"You'll see," Maureen promised mysteriously, and paused to open a set of French doors onto the veranda. As she stepped outside, she called, "Here, Sable!"

A female German shepherd with a coat as black and sleek as its name came loping across the yard, panting a happy grin, tail wagging. Ten roly-poly miniatures tumbled over themselves in an effort to match their mother's gait.

"Puppies!" Tadd squealed in delight and followed Maureen Prescott to the edge of the veranda. The female shepherd washed his face with a single lick before greeting her mistress. Tadd's interest was in the ten little puppies bringing up the rear. "Can I play with them?"

"Of course you may." The instant she gave permission he was racing out to meet the pups. When he knelt on the ground, he was immediately under siege. Valerie joined in with the older woman's laughter as Tadd began giggling in his attempts to elude ten licking tongues. "Puppies and children are made for each other," Maureen declared in a voice breathless from laughter. "Come on, let's sit down and have that drink I promised you. I don't believe Tadd will be interested in lemonade and cookies for a while."

"I'm sure he's forgotten all about it," Valerie agreed, and followed the woman to a white grillwork table with a glass top.

A pitcher of lemonade sat in the center, condensation beading moisture on the outside. Four glasses filled with ice surrounded it as well as a plate of chocolate drop cookies with frosting on the top. Valerie sat down in one of the white iron-lace chairs around the table, plump cushions of green softening the hard seats.

"Tadd is really enjoying himself. The apartment where we live in Cincinnati doesn't permit pets, so this is really a treat for him," Valerie explained, taking the glass of lemonade she was handed and thanking her.

"Misty, my second daughter, lives in a complex that doesn't allow animals, either, and her children are at an age when they want to bring home every stray cat and dog they find. She and her husband have had a time keeping them from sneaking one in. I think their love of animals is part of the reason they come home to Meadow Farms so often. There's Sable and her puppies, the horses, and cats at the barns. But I don't mind what their reason is," Maureen insisted. "I just enjoy having them come. Although it's quite a houseful when they're all here at once."

"Are all your children married?" Valerie asked politely.

"Yes, with the exception of Judd, of course," Maureen answered with a smiling sigh. "There have been times when I've wondered if my firstborn was ever going to get married, but I've never said anything to him."

"I'm sure there are any number of women

who would like to be the one to put an end to your wondering." Valerie was careful not to make it sound as if she was one of them.

"That's the problem — there've been too many women," Maureen Prescott observed with a trace of sad resignation. "The Prescott name, the wealth and his own singular attractiveness — Judd has been the object of many a woman's matrimonial eye. I'm afraid it's made him feel very cynical about the opposite sex."

"I can imagine," Valerie agreed and sipped at the tart, cold liquid in her glass.

"Yes, I've often teased him that I don't know if he's more particular about matching the bloodlines of his thoroughbreds or finding a compatible bloodline for a wife. He always answers that if he ever finds a woman with breeding, spirit and staying power, he'll marry her. Of course, we're only joking," his mother qualified her statement with a dismissing laugh.

Perhaps she had been teasing, but Valerie wouldn't be surprised to discover that Judd wasn't. She knew how cold-blooded he could be about some things . . . and so hot-blooded about others.

Maureen's comment made her wonder whether Judd's mother was subtly trying to warn her that she wasn't good enough for her son. Not that it was needed. Valerie had long been aware of Judd's low opinion of her, an opinion she sometimes forgot, as she had earlier that day. That feeling of unease and a panic to get away came over her again. She had to change the subject away from the discussion of Judd.

Her glance swung over the lawn, including a glimpse of a swimming pool behind some concealing shrubbery. "You must enjoy living here, Mrs. Prescott. It's peaceful, yet with all the conveniences."

"Yes, I love it here," Maureen agreed. "But you must call me Maureen. I learned that there were two requirements to enjoy living here the first year I was married. You have to like country life and you have to *love* horses. Fortunately I managed to fulfill both. The only objection I have is at weaning time when the mares and foals are separated. It tears at my heart to hear them calling back and forth from the pastures to each other. I usually arrange to visit my youngest son, Randall, and his family in Baltimore then. Judd insists that it's silly and impractical to be upset by it, but then he isn't a mother."

The veranda door behind Valerie opened. She glanced over her shoulder, her heart skipping madly against her ribs as Judd's gaze slid warmly over her. Damn, but she couldn't stop loving him, even when she had admitted to herself only a moment ago that it was no good.

Smiling crookedly, he walked to the table. "I told you I wouldn't be long." He glanced to the lawn where Tadd was still playing with the puppies, the black shepherd lying in the grass and looking on. "Tadd is enjoying himself. What have you two been doing?"

"Gossiping about you, of course," his mother replied.

"I didn't realize you gossiped, mother." His comment held a touch of dry mockery.

"I'm human," she said in explanation. "Would you like some lemonade?"

"Yes, I'll have a glass, mother. Thank you." Judd pulled one of the chairs closer to Valerie and sat down. His hand rested on the back of her chair, a finger absently stroking the bare skin of her shoulder. She felt that quivering ache to know the fullness of his caresses and had to move or betray that need.

"Tadd's been so busy playing with the puppies he hasn't had time for lemonade," said Valerie, rising from her chair. "I think I'll see if he wants some now."

Avoiding the glitter of Judd's green eyes,

she walked to the edge of the veranda. All but one of the puppies had grown tired of Tadd's games and had rolled into sleepy balls on the lawn.

"Let the puppies rest for a while, Tadd," she called. "Come and have some lemonade and cookies."

"Okay," he agreed, and stood up, hugging the last puppy in his arms as he started toward the veranda. The mother shepherd rose, made a counting glance at the sleeping litter, and pricked her ears toward Tadd.

"Leave the puppy there, Tadd," Valerie told him. "Its mother wants to keep them all together so they won't accidentally become lost."

Glancing over his shoulder, Tadd saw the anxious black dog looking at him and reluctantly put the puppy onto the grass. The puppy didn't seem sure what it was supposed to do, but its mother trotted over, washed its face and directed it toward the others. Tadd, who seemed to know only one speed, ran to the veranda. He stopped when he reached Valerie, his face aglow, happiness beaming from his expressive hazel green eyes.

"Did you see the puppy? He likes me, mom," he informed her with an eager smile.

"I'm sure he does." She tucked his shirt

inside his pants and brushed at the grass stains on his clothes. Finished, she poked a playful finger at his stomach. "How about some cookies and lemonade for that hole in your tummy?"

"Okay." Tadd skipped alongside of her to the table, hopping onto one of the chairs and resting his elbows on the glass-topped table. Maureen Prescott gave him a glass of lemonade and offered him a cookie. He took one from the plate. "Are all those puppies yours, Reeny?" He used the nickname without hesitation.

"I guess they are," she answered with a smile.

"You're lucky." Tadd took a swallow from the glass as Valerie sat down in her chair, moving it closer to the table to be out of Judd's reach, a fact he noted with a bemused twitch of his mouth. "I wish I could have one puppy," Tadd sighed, and licked at the frosting on the cookie.

"I'm afraid they aren't old enough to leave their mother yet," Maureen Prescott explained.

"Are you going to keep all of them?" His look said that would be greedy.

"No, we'll keep one or two and find good homes for the others," the woman admitted. "But not for another two or three weeks."

"We have a good home, don't we, mom?" Tadd seized on the phrase.

"No, we don't, Tadd," Valerie denied. "Those puppies are going to grow into big dogs like their mother. They need lots of room. Besides, you know that pets aren't allowed where we live."

"Your mother is right," Judd inserted as Tadd twisted his mouth into a grimace. "A puppy needs room to run. You really should live in the country to have a dog like Sable, somewhere like your grandfather's farm. Maybe then your mother would let you have one of the puppies."

Valerie shot him an angry look. She recognized Judd's ploy and resented his using Tadd's desire for a puppy as a wedge to get what he wanted. Tadd latched onto the idea as Judd had known he would.

"But we already live there." He turned an earnest, beseeching look on Valerie.

"Only until the end of the summer," she reminded him.

"Why can't we stay there forever and I could have my puppy," Tadd argued, forgetting the cookie he held.

"But we don't own it." She felt the lazy regard of Judd's green eyes and knew he was enjoying the awkward situation she was in. "Eat your cookie before you make a mess."

"We don't own the apartment in Cincinnati, either," Tadd argued. "So why can't we stay here?"

"Because I have to work. I have a job, remember?" Valerie tried to be patient and reasonable with his demands, knowing she shouldn't release her shortening temper on him.

"No, you don't. You got fired — I heard you tell Clara," he retorted.

"We'll discuss this later, Tadd," she said firmly. "Finish your cookie."

For a minute he opened his mouth to continue his stubborn argument, but the warning look Valerie gave him made him take a bite of the cookie. Tadd was wise enough to know that arousing his mother's temper would accomplish nothing.

"I'm sorry, Valerie," Maureen Prescott sympathized with her dilemma. "It isn't easy to say no to him."

"It isn't," she agreed, and flashed a look at Judd. "But it's a word you learn when you become an adult, sometimes the hard way."

A dark brow flickered upward in a faintly challenging gesture, but Judd gave no other sign that he had received her veiled message. Tadd washed his cookie down with lemonade and turned to Judd.

"Are we going to see Mickey?" he asked.

"Whenever you're ready," Judd conceded.

Tadd hopped off the chair, not even cookies and lemonade keeping him seated for long. "Maybe we can look at the horses, too?" he suggested.

"I think Mickey's planned to show you around and meet the new horses he's looking after." Judd rose from his chair when Valerie did. She avoided the hand that would have taken possession of her arm, and walked to Tadd.

"Thank you for the lemonade and cookies, Mrs. . . . Maureen," she said.

"Yes, thank you," Tadd piped his agreement.

"You're very welcome. And please, come any time," the other woman insisted generously.

"Maybe I could play with the puppies again," Tadd suggested, looking up at Valerie.

"We'll see," she responded stiffly and pushed him forward.

"It's shorter to cut across the lawn," said Judd with a gesture of his hand to indicate the direction they would take.

Despite Valerie's efforts to keep Tadd at her side, he skipped into the lead and she was forced to walk with Judd. She was aware of the way he shortened his long strides to match hers. He made no attempt at conversation, letting his nearness wreak havoc on her senses.

At the barns, they had no trouble finding Mickey. He appeared from one of them as they arrived. He hurried toward them, his bowed legs giving a slight waddle to his walk. Tadd ran forward to meet him.

"Hello, Valerie. How have you been?" Mickey greeted her with his usual face-splitting grin.

"Fine," she responded, a little of her tension easing. "Tadd has missed you."

"I've missed him, too." Mickey glanced down at the boy holding his hand. "Come on, lad. I want you to see some of the finest-looking horseflesh there is in this part of the world. You've got to learn to know a great horse when you see one if you want to work with horses when you grow up."

"I do." Tadd trotted eagerly beside him as Mickey turned to retrace his path to the stable. "I'm going to have a lot of animals when I grow up — horses and dogs and everything."

Valerie followed them with Judd remaining at her side. She glanced at his jutting profile through the sweep of her gold-tipped lashes. The hard sensuality of his features attracted her despite her anger.

"It wasn't fair of you to tempt Tadd with the prospect of a puppy," she protested in a low, agitated breath.

Judd's gaze slid lazily down to her face. "All's fair," he countered smoothly.

In the shade of the stable overhang, Valerie stopped. "The end does not justify the means," she said sharply.

Judd stopped, looking down at her in a way that heated her flesh. "You can justify any means if you want something badly enough — and you know what I want."

The message in his eyes seemed to cut off her breath. She could feel the powerful undertow of desire tugging at her, threatening to drag her under the control of his will. She seemed powerless to resist.

Farther down the stable row, Tadd glanced over his shoulder at the couple lagging behind, "Mom, are you coming?" he called.

Her breath came in a rush of self-consciousness.

"Yes, Tadd," she answered, and turned to catch up with them.

"You can't run away from it," Judd's low voice mocked her disguised flight. He lingered for an instant, then leisurely moved to follow her.

CHAPTER EIGHT

The quartet led by Mickey Flanners had made almost a full tour of the brood farm, impressive in its efficiency. Nothing had been overlooked, especially in the foaling barn, a facility that Valerie was sure had no equal.

The tour had paused at a paddock fence where Tadd had climbed to the top rail to watch a pair of galloping yearlings cavorting and kicking up their heels. From the stud barns came the piercing squeal of a stallion answered by the challenging scream of a second. Valerie glanced toward the sound, noticing Judd had done the same.

A frown flickered across his face, followed by a crooked smile of dismissal. "It sounds as if Battleground and King's Ruler are at it again. They're always feuding with each other across the way."

Valerie nodded in silent understanding. Stallions were often jealously competitive. The instinct within them to fight to protect their territory was strong, which was why they had to be kept separated by the strongest of fences. With Judd's explanation echoing in her mind, she ignored the angry exchange of whistles that had resumed.

A muffled shout of alarm pivoted Judd around. More shouts were followed by a flurry of activity around the stud barn. A grimness claimed his expression.

"I'll be back," he said without glancing at her.

His long, ground-eating strides were already covering the distance to the stallion pens before either Valerie or Mickey thought to move. Tadd followed curiously after them, sensing something different in the air.

When Valerie reached the barrier of the first stud pen, she felt the first sickening jolt of danger. The two stallions were locked in combat, rearing, jaws open and heads snaking for each other's jugular vein. The clang of pawing steel hooves striking against each other vibrated in the air amid the blowing snorts and rumbling neighs. Stable hands were warily trying to separate the pair. The blood drained from her face as she saw Judd wading into the thick of it.

"Stop him, Mickey!" she breathed to the ex-jockey beside her.

"Are you crazy?" he asked in disbelief. "Judd isn't going to stand by and watch his two prize stallions kill each other."

She could hear him snapping orders to coordinate the efforts. Fear for his safety overpowered her and she turned away. "I can't watch." Valerie knew what those murderous hooves could do. They were capable of tearing away hunks of human flesh, exposing the bones. "Tell me what happens, Mickey." She closed her eyes, but she couldn't shut her ears to the sounds. "No, I don't want to know," she groaned, and remembered Tadd.

She reached for him, trying to hide his face from the sight, but he tore out of her arms. "I want to see, mommy!" he cried fearlessly, and raced to Mickey's side.

Valerie felt sick with fear. The turmoil within the stud pen seemed to go on without end. Her eyes were tightly closed, her back to the scene as she prayed desperately that Judd would be unharmed. She hadn't the strength for anything else. Fear had turned her into jelly.

"Hot damn! He did it!" Mickey shouted, and danced a little jig, stopping at the sight of Valerie's ashen face as she collapsed weakly against a fence post. "Hey, Valerie —" his voice was anxious with concern "— it's over."

"Judd . . . ?" was all she could manage as a violent trembling seized her.

"He's fine." Mickey said it as though she shouldn't have thought otherwise. Tipping his head to one side, he looked up at her, smiling in gentle understanding. "You're still in love with him, aren't you?" he commented.

She nodded her head in a numbed, affirmative gesture before catching the phrasing of his question. "How . . ." she began, but her choked voice didn't seem to want to work.

"I noticed all those rides you were taking seven years ago and the look that was in your eyes when you came back. I knew a man put it there," Mickey explained softly. "And I happened to notice that Judd was taking rides the same time you were. I just put two and two together." At the apprehensive light in her eyes, he answered her unspoken question. "Your grandad didn't know and I didn't see where it was my place to enlighten him. There was enough grief around the place after you left without adding to it."

A shuddering sense of gratitude rippled through her and she smiled weakly. Her stomach had finally begun to stop its nauseous churning, but her legs were still treacherously weak. She gripped the fence tightly for support as Mickey turned away.

She didn't guess why until she heard Judd's grim voice speaking as he approached them.

"I've fired that new man, Rathburn. The stupid fool had to clean King's paddock, so he put the stallion in the one next to Battleground and didn't check the gates," Judd said with ruthless scorn for the guilty man's incompetence. "Battleground has some wicked-looking cuts. The vet is on his way, but you'd better see if you can give Jim a hand, Mick."

"Right away." The ex-jockey moved off at a shuffling trot.

"That was really something!" Tadd breathed in excitement.

"Is that right?" Judd's mocking voice sounded tolerantly amused.

Valerie didn't find anything humorous about the near disaster that could have ultimately crippled horse and man. Glancing over her shoulder, she cast Judd an accusing look, her face still white as a sheet. His white shirt was stained with dirt and sweat, and a telltale scattering of animal hairs showed he had put himself in equal danger as his stable hands.

"You could have been killed or maimed!" A thin thread of her previous fear ran through her hoarse voice.

His gaze narrowed on her in sharp concern. "You look like a ghost, Valerie," Judd concluded in his own accusation. "Quick, Tadd, run and get your mother some water."

His hand gripped the boy's shoulder and sent him speeding on his way. Then he was walking to her. Valerie turned toward the fence, relieved that he had come away unscathed, frightened by what might have happened, and weak with her love for him. His hands spanned her waist to turn her from the fence and receive the complacent study of his gaze.

"As many times as you've wished me to hell, I would have thought you would relish the prospect of my death," Judd taunted her.

"No," Valerie denied, and protested painfully, "That's a cruel thing to say!"

"Why? Do you really care what happens to me?" His voice was dry and baiting.

"I do." What was the use in denying it? Her downcast gaze noticed the smear of red blood on the sleeve of his shirt. It was horse blood. At the sight of it, her hands spread across his chest to feel the steady beat of his heart. She swayed against him, the side of her cheek brushing against the hair-roughened chest where his shirt was unbuttoned. She wished she could absorb some of his indomitable strength. "I don't want to care, but I do," Valerie admitted in an aching breath.

His arms tightened around her in a crushing circle. The force of it tipped her head back and his mouth bruised her cheekbone. "You're mine, Valerie," he growled in possession. "You belong to me."

"Yes," she agreed to the inevitable.

"There'll be no more talk about you leaving in September," Judd warned.

"No." Valerie surrendered to his demand.

With that final acquiescence, his mouth sought and found her parted lips. He kissed her deeply, savoring this moment when she had yielded to his will and admitted what she couldn't hide. He stirred her to passion, creating a languorous flame that ravished her. She molded herself to his length, to fire his blood as he had hers. The sudden bruising demand of his mouth consoled her that he couldn't resist her, either.

"Mommy?" Tadd's anxious voice tore her lips from the satisfaction of Judd's kiss. Her dazed eyes focused slowly on the small boy running toward them. "Reeny's bringing the water. Is mommy all right?"

Judd's bulk was shielding Valerie from the view of both the boy and the woman hurrying behind him. With shuddering reluctance Judd relaxed his hold to let her feet rest firmly on the ground, instead of just her toes. His green eyes blazed over her face in promise and possession, letting her see he didn't welcome the interruption before he turned to meet it. A supporting arm remained curved across her back and waist, keeping her body in contact with his side.

"What's happened, Judd?" His mother hurried forward, a glass of water in her hand. Her gaze flicked from her son to Valerie, and Valerie guessed that Maureen Prescott had recognized that embrace for what it had been. She flushed self-consciously. "I heard an uproar down around the stallion barns, then Tadd came running to the house talking about horses fighting and Valerie needing water. I didn't know whether to listen to him or call an ambulance."

Judd explained briefly about the stallion fight, glossing over his part in it, and concluded, "It left Valerie a little shaken, so I sent Tadd to the house as an excuse to get him away. I thought she was going to faint and I didn't want that scaring him." He took the glass from his mother's hand and offered it to Valerie. "You might want that drink now, though."

"Thank you." Nervously she took the glass and sipped from it, too self-conscious about the scene his mother had witnessed to draw attention to herself by refusing his suggestion.

"Do you feel all right now, Valerie?" Maureen asked with concern.

"Yes, I'm fine." But her voice sounded breathless and not altogether sure.

"You look a little pale," the other woman observed, frowning anxiously. "You'd better come up to the house and rest for a few minutes."

"No, really I —" Valerie tried to protest.

But Judd interrupted. "Do you want me to carry you?"

"No, I . . . I can walk," she stammered, and flashed a nervous glance at his mother.

Incapable of conversation, Valerie was relieved that no one seemed to expect any from her as they walked to the house. Judd's arm remained around her, his thigh brushing against hers. She kept wondering what his mother was thinking and whether she objected to what was apparently going on. But she guessed that Maureen Prescott was too polite and well-bred to let her feelings show.

As they crossed the lawn to the veranda, Tadd began his own description of the scene at the stud pens. "Mickey and I were watching it all, Reeny. You should have seen Judd when he —"

Judd must have felt the slight tremor that vibrated through her. "I think that's enough about that, Tadd," he silenced the boy. "We don't want to upset your mother again, do we?"

"No," Tadd agreed, darting an anxious look at Valerie.

"Why don't you play with the puppies, Tadd?" Maureen suggested, and he wandered toward the sleeping pile of black fur, but with some reluctance.

"I'm sorry." Valerie felt obliged to apologize for her behavior after she came under the scrutiny of Judd's mother, as well. "I'm not usually a fraidycat about such things."

"No, you're not," Judd agreed with a gently taunting smile, and escorted her to a cushioned lounge chair. "A spitting feline, maybe," he qualified.

"There's no need to apologize, Valerie," his mother inserted. "I saw a stallion fight once. It was a vicious thing, so I quite understand your reaction."

"Comfortable?" Judd inquired after seating her in the chair.

"Yes." But she was beginning to feel like a fraud.

"You relax for a little while," he ordered. "I'm going to wash up and change my shirt," he said, glancing down at his soiled front. "I won't be long."

When he had disappeared into the house via the veranda doors, his mother suggested, "There's some lemonade left if you'd like some."

"No, thank you," Valerie refused.

Tadd came wandering back onto the veranda, a sleepy-eyed puppy in his arms. He stopped at the lounge chair, studying Valerie with a troubled light in his eyes.

"Are you all right, mommy?"

His appealing concern drew a faint smile. "Yes, Tadd, I'm fine," she assured him.

"Maybe you'd feel better if you held the puppy." He offered her the soft ball of fur with enormous feet.

"Thanks, Tadd, but I think the puppy would like it better if you held it," Valerie refused, her heart warming at his touching gesture.

"It's sleepy anyway," he shrugged, and walked over to the grass to let it go. "Would you want to play a game, mom?"

"No, thanks."

He came back over to her chair. "What am I going to do while you're resting?" he wanted to know.

"Would you like some more cookies and lemonade?" Maureen Prescott suggested.

"No, thank you." He half turned to look at her. "Have you got any more animals for me to play with?"

"No, I don't believe so." The woman tried not to smile at the question. "But there's a sandbox over by those trees. If I'm not mistaken, there's a toy truck in that chest over there. You can take the truck and play with it in the sandbox."

"Great!" Tadd dashed to the toy chest she had indicated, retrieved the truck and headed for the sandbox.

"Tadd isn't used to entertaining himself," Valerie explained. "There are a lot of children his age in the apartment building where we live, so he's used to playing with them."

"It's good that he has children to play with," Maureen commented.

"Yes," Valerie agreed. "I think that's the only thing he's missed this summer. Mickey played with him at the farm a lot. Now that he's gone, Tadd gets lonely once in a while."

"Ellie, my eldest daughter, is coming this weekend with her husband and their six-year-old daughter. Meg is a regular tomboy. Why don't you bring Tadd over Sunday afternoon?" Maureen suggested. "They'll have fun playing together."

"I . . . I don't think so." Valerie hesitated before rejecting the invitation.

"Please try," the woman urged.

"Try what?" Judd appeared, catching the tail end of their conversation.

"I suggested to Valerie that she bring Tadd over on Sunday to play with Meg, but she doesn't think she'll be able to," his mother explained.

"Oh?" His gaze flicked curiously to Valerie. "Why?"

"I'm not sure it will be possible yet. I'll have to speak to Clara." Valerie couldn't explain the reason for her hesitation. She had the feeling it wouldn't be wise to become too closely involved with any more members of the Prescott family.

"Don't worry, mother," said Judd. "I can almost guarantee you that Tadd will be here. Valerie and I are having dinner together on Saturday night. I'll persuade her to change her mind."

Dinner together? It was the first she knew about it, but she tried not to let on. Things were happening at such a rapid pace that she couldn't keep up with them. She needed time to take stock of things and understand what was going on.

"I hope you will," his mother said. "Tadd is a wonderful boy. You must be very proud of him, Valerie."

"I am," Valerie admitted, feeling vaguely uncomfortable again.

"He has such an appealing face." Maureen was looking toward the sandbox in which Tadd was playing with the truck. "And those eyes of his are so expressive. There's something about him that makes him so very special, but those children generally are," she concluded.

"Those children?" Valerie stiffened.

A pair of turquoise eyes rounded in dismay as Maureen realized what she had said. She glanced quickly at Judd, an apology in her look. Valerie's questioning eyes were directed at him, as well.

Undaunted by either of them, he replied smoothly, "I believe mother means those children who are born out of wedlock."

"I'm sorry, Valerie," Maureen apologized. "I didn't mean to offend you by that remark — truly I didn't."

"It's quite all right." Valerie hid her embarrassment behind a proud look. "I've never attempted to hide the fact that Tadd is illegitimate. And I have heard it said that 'those children' tend to be more precious and appealing as a result. Tadd seems to be an example of that, but I doubt if it's always the case."

"I certainly didn't mean to hurt your feelings," Maureen insisted again. "It's just that I've been watching Tadd," she rushed her explanation, "and he's so like Judd in many ways that — Oh, dear, I've made it worse!" she exclaimed as she looked into Valerie's whitened face.

"No, no," Valerie denied with a tight, strained smile. "I understand perfectly."

A nauseous lump was rising in her throat as she truly began to understand. Maureen Prescott had known all along that her son was Tadd's father. Judd had obviously told his mother, but hadn't bothered to tell Valerie that he had. She hadn't thought it was possible to feel cheap and humiliated again, but she did.

"I didn't see any reason not to tell her," Judd explained, watching Valerie through narrowed eyes.

"Of course there isn't," she agreed, feeling her poise cracking and struggling inwardly to keep it from falling apart.

"I'm relieved." His mother smiled, somewhat nervously. "And I do hope it won't influence your decision about bringing Tadd here on Sunday. I would sincerely enjoy having him come."

"Don't worry about that, mother," Judd inserted. "I'm sure Valerie will agree."

"Your son can be very persuasive," Valerie commented, and felt a rising well of panic. "I don't mean to be rude, Mrs. Prescott —" she rose from the lounge chair "— but I'm really not feeling all that well. Would you mind if Judd took us home now? You've been very gracious to Tadd and me and I want to thank you for that."

"You're very welcome, of course," Maureen returned, hiding her confusion with a smile. "I'll call Tadd for you."

"Thank you." Valerie was aware of Judd standing beside her, examining the pallor in her face.

"What's wrong, Valerie?" he asked quietly.

"A headache — a nervous reaction, I suppose." Her temples were throbbing, so her excuse wasn't totally false.

He seemed to accept her surface explanation without delving further. When Tadd came racing to the veranda, Maureen Prescott walked them through the house to the front door and bid them goodbye. As they drove away, Tadd's face was pressed to the window glass to watch the horses in the pasture.

Valerie sat silently in the front seat. Judd

slid her a questioning look. "Does it bother you that mother knows?" he asked, phrasing it so Tadd wouldn't attach any significance to it.

"No." She leaned her head against the seat rest. "Why should it?" she countered with forced nonchalance.

But it beat at her like a hammer. To realize that her relationship with Judd was out in the open was worse than if it had been a secret, clandestine affair. Kept woman, mistress, consort — all were terms for the same thing. She had agreed to it — in the stable yard in Judd's arms. There was no doubt about how deeply she loved him.

But she had more to think of than just herself. There was Tadd. Valerie closed her eyes in pain. Maureen Prescott was eager for him to visit on Sunday, but the invitation naturally hadn't included her. Was Tadd going to grow up on the fringes of the Prescott family, invited into the circle on their whim? He would be a Prescott without a right to the name. How would he feel when he discovered the truth? Would he become bitter and resentful that his mother was the mistress of the man who was his father?

Valerie was tormented by the love she felt for Judd and the life with him that she never could know. It gnawed at her until she thought she would be torn in two. It was a searing, raw ache that made her heart bleed.

"Valerie?" Judd's hand touched her shoulder.

She opened her eyes to discover the car was parked in front of the farmhouse. The screen door was already slamming behind Tadd, who was racing into the house to be the first to tell Clara of all that had happened that day.

"I . . . I didn't realize we were here already," Valerie began in painful confusion.

"I noticed," he responded dryly. His hand slid under her hair, discovering the tense muscles in her neck and massaging them. "You do know you're having dinner with me on Saturday night, tomorrow night," he told her.

"So you told me." She couldn't relax under his touch; if anything, she became stiffer.

"You're going." It was a statement that demanded her agreement.

"Yes," Valerie lied because it was easier.

Judd leaned over and rubbed his mouth against the corner of her lips. She breathed in sharply, filling her lungs with the scent of him. It was like a heady wine. Judd began nibbling the curve of her lip, teasing and tantalizing her with his kiss.

"Please, Judd, don't!" She turned her head away from his tempting mouth because she knew the power of his kiss could make her forget everything.

He hooked a hard finger around her chin and turned her to face him. His sharp gaze inspected her pale face and the carefully lowered lashes.

"What is it?" He sensed something was wrong and demanded to know the cause.

"I really do have a headache," Valerie insisted with a nervous smile. "It'll go away, but I need to lie down for a while."

"Alone?" His brow quirked suggestively, then he sighed, "Never mind. Forget I said that. I'll call you later to be sure you're all right."

"Make it this evening," Valerie asked quickly, and hurried to answer the question in his eyes. "By the time I rest for an hour or two, it'll be time to eat. Then there's the dishes to be done, and Tadd won't take a bath unless someone is standing over him. So I'll be busy until . . ." His fingers touched her lips to silence them.

"I'll phone you later this evening," he agreed. "Or I'll come over if you can think of a way to get that battle-ax out of the house."

It was starting already, she thought in panic. "You'd better call first," she said.

"Very well, I will." He kissed her lightly.

CHAPTER NINE

Valerie paused on the porch to wave to Judd and stayed until he had driven out of sight down the lane. She felt the beginning of a sob in her throat and knew she didn't have time for tears. Lifting her chin, she turned and walked into the house.

"My gracious, it certainly sounds as if you've had a full day," Clara commented. "Tadd has been running nonstop for the last five minutes and doesn't give any indication of wearing down. What's all this about horses and puppies? I thought you were going to a tobacco auction. That's what you told me."

"We did go," Valerie admitted, "but that was earlier today. Then we went over to the Prescott place to see Mickey." She glanced down at her son. "Tadd, why don't you go outside and play for a while?"

"Aw, mom," he protested, "I wanted to tell Clara about the puppies."

"Later," she insisted. Reluctantly Tadd walked to the door, his feet dragging, and slammed the screen shut. Valerie turned to Clara. "How much gas is in the car?"

"I filled it up the other day when I was in town. Why?" Clara was startled by the question.

Valerie was already hurrying through the living room, picking up the odds and ends of personal items that had managed to become scattered around. She began stuffing them in a paper sack.

"What about the oil? Did you have it checked?" she asked.

"As a matter of fact, I did." A pair of hands moved to rest on broad hips. "Would you mind telling me why you're asking these questions?"

Valerie stopped in the center of the room, pressing a hand against her forehead. "I can't remember — did we put the suitcases in the empty bedroom upstairs or down in the basement?"

"Upstairs. And what do we need the suitcases for?" Clara followed as Valerie headed for the staircase.

"Because we're leaving. What other reason would I have for asking about the car and suitcases?" Valerie retorted sharply.

"Would you like to run that by me once more? Did I hear you say we were leaving?" repeated Clara.

"That's exactly what I said." Valerie opened the door to the empty bedroom, grabbed two of the suitcases in the corner, and walked to Tadd's room.

"I thought we were staying here until summer was over," her friend reminded her.

"I've changed my mind. Isn't it obvious?" Valerie opened drawers, taking out whole stacks of clothes regardless of their order or neatness, and jamming them into the opened suitcase.

"Suppose you give me three guesses as to why?" Clara challenged. "Judd Prescott, Judd Prescott, and Judd Prescott. What happened today?"

"I don't have time to go into it right now," Valerie stalled. "Would you mind helping me pack?" she demanded. "I don't want to take all night."

"I'll help," Clara replied, walking to the closet without any degree of haste. "But I doubt if what you're doing could be called packing. What's the big rush anyway? You surely aren't planning to leave tonight?" Shrewd blue eyes swept piercingly to Valerie.

"We're leaving tonight." The first suitcase was filled to the point of overflowing. Valerie had to sit on it to get it latched. "We'll never be able to put everything in these suitcases. Where are the boxes your sister used to send our things? We didn't throw them away, did we?"

But her friend was still concentrating on her first statement. "Tonight? You can't mean to leave tonight?" She frowned. "There's only a few hours of daylight left. The sensible thing is to leave first thing in the morning."

"No, it isn't," Valerie argued. "We're leaving tonight. Now where are the boxes?"

"Forget the boxes. I want to know why we have to leave tonight. And I'm not answering another question or lifting a hand until you tell me." Clara dropped the clothes in her hand on a chair.

"Clara, for heaven's sake, I don't have time for all this." Valerie hurried to the chair and grabbed the clothes to stuff them in the second suitcase. "Judd will be calling later on and I want to be gone before he does."

"And that's your reason?" Her friend sniffed in scoffing challenge. "It seems mighty ridiculous to me!"

"Don't you understand?" Valerie whirled to face her. The conflicting emotions and raw pain that she had pushed aside now threatened to surface. Her chin quivered as she fought to hold them back. "If I don't leave tonight, I never will!"

"I think you'd better sit down and tell me what's happened," said Clara in a voice that would stand for no argument.

"No, I won't sit down." Valerie sniffed away a tear and shook back her caramel hair. "There's too much to do and not enough time." She walked to the chest of drawers and opened the last one to take out the balance of clothes.

"Well, you're going to tell me what happened," Clara insisted.

Another tear was forming in the corner of her eye and Valerie wiped it quickly away with a forefinger. "Judd's mother, Mrs. Prescott, knows about Tadd, that Judd is his father. She wants Tadd to come over on Sunday to play with another one of her grandchildren. It's all out in the open, and I can't handle it."

"What is Judd's reaction to this?" Clara gathered up Tadd's few toys and put them in a sack.

"He told his mother he would persuade me to bring Tadd."

"So? Don't let him persuade you," her friend suggested with a shrug.

Valerie's laugh held no humor. "All he has to do is hold me in his arms and I'll agree to anything. I did today. I promised I wouldn't leave here. I'm so in love with him

I'm losing my pride and my self-respect."

"It isn't one-sided. Judd is absolutely besotted with you," Clara said. "I've seen the way he watches you. He never takes his eyes off you. He knows when you blink or take a breath."

"I know and it doesn't make it any easier. Clara, he wants me to become his. . . ." She broke off the sentence with a hurtful sigh. "I can't even say the word without thinking what it would ultimately do to Tadd."

"Maybe he'll marry you," Clara suggested in an effort to comfort her.

Valerie shook her head, pressing her lips tightly together for an instant. "I'm not good enough for a Prescott to marry. I lack breeding," she said bitterly. "I can't stay, Clara." Her hands absently wadded the bundle of clothes in her hand, her fingers digging into the material. "I can't stay."

There was silence. Then a detergent-roughened hand gently touched her shoulder. "The boxes are in my bedroom closet. I'll get them."

"Thank you, Clara," Valerie muttered in a voice tight and choked with emotion.

When the two suitcases were packed, she set them at the head of the stairs and took two more to her bedroom. With Clara's help, all her personal belongings were packed in either the luggage or the cardboard shipping crates. As soon as that room was cleared of their possessions they started on Clara's. No time was wasted on neatness or order.

"All that's left is to lug all this downstairs and out to the car," said Clara, taking a deep breath as she studied the pile of luggage and boxes in front of the staircase.

"And to check downstairs," Valerie added, picking up one case and juggling another under the same arm. "We'd better be sure to get everything because I'm not coming back no matter what we leave behind," she declared grimly, and reached for the third.

Leading the way, Valerie descended the stairs. Clara followed with one of the boxes. Tadd came bounding onto the porch as Valerie approached the door.

"Open the door for me, Tadd," she called through the wire mesh.

"I'm tired of playing, mom." He held the door open for her and stared curiously at the suitcase she carried. "What are you doing? Are you going somewhere?"

"Yes. Don't let go of the door; Clara is right behind me," Valerie rushed when she saw him take a step to follow her.

"Hurry up, Clara." Tadd waited impatiently for the stout woman to maneuver the box through the opening, then let the door slam and raced to catch up to Valerie. "Is Clara going, too?"

"We're all going," Valerie answered, and set the cases on the ground next to the car. "Where are the keys for the trunk, Clara? Are they in the ignition?"

"I'll bet they're in the house in my handbag," the woman grumbled, and set the box beside the luggage. "Stay here. I'll go and get them."

"Where are we going, mom?" Tadd wanted to know, tugging at her skirt to get her attention.

"We're going home," she told him, only Cincinnati didn't seem like home anymore. This place was home.

"Home? To Cincinnati?" Tadd frowned.

"Yes. Back to our apartment," Valerie answered sharply.

"Is summer over already?" His expression was both puzzled and crestfallen, a sad light in his eyes.

"No, not quite," she admitted, and glanced to the house. What was keeping Clara? Valerie could have been bringing out more of the boxes herself instead of standing there.

"But I thought we were going to stay here

until summer was over," Tadd reminded her. "That's what you said."

"I changed my mind." *Please,* Valerie thought desperately, *I don't want to argue with you.*

"Why are we leaving?" he asked. "If summer isn't over, why do we have to go back?"

"Because I said we are." She wasn't about to explain the reasons to him. In the first place, he wouldn't understand. And in the second, it would be too painful. The breeze whipped a strand of hair across her cheek and she pushed it away with an impatient gesture.

"But I don't want to go back," Tadd protested in a petulant tone.

"Yes, you do," Valerie insisted.

"No, I don't." His mouth was pulled into a mutinous pout.

"What about all your friends?" Valerie attempted to reason with him. "Wouldn't you like to go back and play with them? It's been quite a while since you've ridden on Mike's Big Wheels. That was a lot of fun, remember?"

"I don't care about Mike's dumb old Big Wheels," Tadd grumbled, the pouting mouth growing more pronounced. "It's not nearly as much fun as riding Ginger, anyway. I want to stay here."

"We're not going to stay here. We're leaving. We're going back to Cincinnati." Valerie stressed each sentence with decisive emphasis. "So you might as well get that straight right now."

"I don't want to go," he repeated, his voice raised in rebellious protest. "Judd said if we lived here, maybe I could have a puppy."

"I'm not going to listen to any more talk about puppies!" Valerie retorted, her nerves snapping under the strain of his persistent arguing. "We're leaving, and that's final!"

"Well, I'm not going!" Tadd shouted, backing away and breaking into angry tears.

"Tadd." Valerie immediately regretted her sharpness, but he was already turning away and running toward the pasture. She could hear his sobbing. "Tadd, come back here!"

But he ignored the command, his little legs churning faster. He was running into the lowering sun. Valerie shaded her eyes with her hand to shield out the glaring light. She waited for him to stop at the paddock fence, but instead he scooted under it and kept running.

"Tadd, come back here!" she called anxiously.

"I've got the keys," Clara came out of the house, dangling the car keys in front of her. "I couldn't remember where I had left my handbag. I finally found it underneath the kitchen table. If it were a snake, it would have bit me."

"Would you pack all this in the trunk?" Valerie motioned to the luggage as she started toward the pasture. "I'd better get Tadd."

"Where's he gone?" Frowning, Clara glanced around the yard, missing the small figure racing across the pasture.

"I lost my temper with him because he said he didn't want to go," Valerie explained. "Now he's run off."

"Let him be." Clara dismissed any urgency to the situation with a wave of her hand. "He's just going to sulk for a while. He'll be back. Meanwhile, he won't be underfoot."

"I don't know. . . ." Valerie answered hesitantly.

"He won't go far," the other woman assured her as she walked to the car to unlock the trunk and begin arranging the luggage and boxes inside.

"He was very upset." Gazing across, she could see Tadd had stopped running and was leaning against a tree to cry.

"Of course he was upset," Clara agreed in a voice that disdainfully dismissed any other thought. "All children get upset when they don't get their way. You go right ahead and handle the situation any way you want. I don't want to be telling you how you should raise your kid."

Valerie received her friend's subtle message that she was making a mountain out of a molehill and sighed, "You may be right."

"If you're not going after him, you could give me a hand with some of this stuff. You're the one who was in such an all-fired hurry to leave," came the gruff reminder. Then Clara muttered to herself, "I get the feeling we're making our getaway after robbing a bank."

When another glance at the pasture showed that Tadd was in the same place, Valerie hesitated an instant longer, then turned to help Clara with the luggage. A second trip into the house brought everything down from upstairs.

A search of the ground floor added a box of belongings. Valerie carried it to the car. Her gaze swung automatically to the paddock, but this time there was no sign of Tadd. She walked to the fence and called him. The bay mare lifted its head in answer, then went back to grazing.

What had been merely concern changed to worry as Valerie hesitantly retraced her steps to the house. The sounds coming from the kitchen located Clara for her. She walked quickly to that room.

"You haven't seen Tadd, have you?" she asked hopefully. "He isn't in the pasture anymore and I thought he might have slipped into the house."

"I haven't seen hide nor hair of him." Clara shook her wiry, frosted gray hair. "Would you look at all this food? It seems a shame to leave it."

"We don't have much choice. It would spoil if we tried to take it with us." Valerie's response was automatic. "Where do you suppose Tadd is?"

"Probably somewhere around the barns." The dismissing lift of Clara's wide shoulders indicated that she still believed he wasn't far away. "Since we haven't had any supper, I'll fix some sandwiches and snacks to take along with us. That way we'll get to use up some of this food and not leave so much behind."

"I'm going to check the barns to see if Tadd is there," Valerie said with an uneasy feeling growing inside her.

A walk through the barns proved fruitless and her calls went unanswered. She hurried back to the house to tell Clara.

"He wasn't there," she said with a trace of breathless panic.

"The little imp!" Clara wiped her hands on a towel. "He's probably off hiding somewhere."

"Well, we can't leave without him," Valerie said, as if Clara had foolishly implied that they would. "I'm going to walk out to the pasture where I saw him last."

"I'll check through the house to make sure he didn't sneak in here when we weren't looking." Clara put aside the food she was preparing for the trip and started toward the other rooms.

While Clara began a search of the house, Valerie hurried to the paddock. She ducked between the fence rails and walked swiftly through the tall grass to the tree on the far side of the pasture where she had last seen Tadd.

"Tadd!" She stopped when she reached the tree and used it as a pivot point to make a sweeping arc of the surrounding country. "Tadd, where are you?" A bird chattered loudly in the only response she received. "Tadd, answer me!" Her voice rose, on a desperate note.

From the point of the tree there was a faint trail angling away from it, barely discernible by the tall, thick grass that had been pushed down by running feet. The vague path seemed to be heading in the opposite direction from the house. It was the only clue Valerie had and she followed it.

It lead her to the boundary fence with Meadow Farms and beyond. Halfway across the adjoining pasture, the grass thinned. Grazing horses had cropped the blades too close to the ground. She lost the trail that had taken her this far, and stopped, looking around for any hint that would tell her which direction Tadd had gone.

"Tadd, where are you going?" she muttered, wishing she could crawl inside her young son's mind and discover his intention.

Did he know he had crossed onto the home farm of the Prescotts? It didn't seem likely. Despite the time they had spent there, Tadd wasn't familiar with the area beyond the farm and its immediate pastures. Yet it was possible that he knew the general direction of Meadow Farms main quarters.

But why would he go there? To see Judd and enlist his support to persuade her to stay? No, Valerie dismissed that idea. Tadd was too young to think in such terms. The idea of finding Judd wouldn't lead him to the Prescott house, but the puppies might.

Hoping that she was reading his mind, she set off in the general direction of the Meadow Farms' buildings. Her pace quickened with her growing desire to find Tadd before he reached his destination. The last thing her panicking heart wanted was a confrontation with Judd. She had to find Tadd before he found the puppies and Judd.

As she crossed the meadow, Valerie caught herself biting her lip. There was painful constriction in her chest and her breath was coming in half sobs. It did no good to try to calm her trembling nerves.

The ground rumbled with the pounding of galloping hooves and she glanced up to see Judd on the gray hunter riding toward her. She looked around for somewhere to hide, but it was too late. He had already seen her. Besides, she had to know if he had found Tadd, regardless of whether Judd had learned of her intention to leave. At the moment, finding Tadd was more important.

Judd didn't slow his horse until he was almost up to her. He dismounted before it came to a full stop. Then his long strides carried him swiftly toward her, holding the reins in his hand and leading the horse to her.

"Have you seen Tadd?" Her worried gaze searched his grimly set features. "He ran off and I can't find him."

"I know," said Judd, and explained tersely, "I phoned the house a few minutes ago to find out how you were feeling and Clara told me Tadd was missing." His large hand took hold of her arm and started to pull her toward the horse. "Come on."

"No!" Valerie struggled in panic. "You don't understand. I have to find Tadd," she protested frantically.

If Judd hadn't seen Tadd, it meant he was still out there somewhere, possibly lost. The shadows cast by the sun were already long. Soon it would be dusk. She had to find him before darkness came, and there was a lot of ground yet to be covered. That knowledge made her resist Judd's attempt to take her with him all the more wildly.

"Dammit, Valerie. Stop it! You're coming with me," Judd snapped with savage insistence. Her arms became captured by the iron grip of his hands.

"No, I won't!" she protested violently. "I won't!"

A hard shake jarred her into silence. "Will you listen to me?" His angry face was close to hers, his eyes glittering into hers in hard demand. "I have a feeling," he said tightly.

"I think I know where Tadd is. Now, will you come with me or do I have to throw you over my shoulder and take you with me?"

Tears of panic had begun to scorch her eyes. She blinked at them and nodded her head mutely. But Judd didn't alter his hold. He seemed determined to hear her voice an agreement before he believed her.

"I . . . I'll come with y-you." She managed to force out a shaky agreement.

His hands shifted their grip from her arms to her waist. He lifted her up to sit sideways on the front of the saddle. Then he swung up behind her, his arms circling her to hold the reins and guide the gray.

The horse lunged into a canter, throwing Valerie against Judd's chest. The arm around her waist tightened to offer support. The solidness of his chest offered comfort and strength. Valerie let herself relax against it. She hadn't realized how heavy the weight of concern had been for Tadd's whereabouts until Judd had taken on half of the burden.

Through the cotton skirt of her sun dress she could feel the hard muscles of his thighs. Her gaze swept up to study his face through the curl of her gold-tipped lashes. The jutting angle of his jaw and the line of his mouth were set with grim purpose. He slowed the horse as they entered a grouping of trees and wound their way through them.

As if feeling her look, he glanced down and the light in his green eyes became softly mocking. "When you were spitting at me in all your fury, did you really believe I was going to try to keep you from finding our son?"

"I didn't know," Valerie answered, uncertain now as to what she had believed his intention was.

"I guess I have given you cause in the past to question my motives," Judd admitted.

"Sometimes," she agreed, but she didn't question them now.

His gaze was drawn beyond her and he reined in the gray. "Look," he instructed quietly.

Valerie turned and saw a familiar grassy clearing. They had stopped on the edge of it. In the middle of it, a small figure lay on his stomach, a position in which Tadd had cried himself to sleep.

Her gaze lifted in stunned wonderment to Judd's face. "How?" she whispered.

"I can't begin to explain it." He shook his head with a similar expression of awed confusion mixed with quiet acceptance of the fact. His gaze wandered gently back to hers. "Any more than I can explain how I knew Tadd would be here."

Valerie remembered stories of the salmon finding their way back to their spawning grounds and wondered if Tadd possessed that same mysterious instinct in order to be led here. It was a miracle that filled her with a glowing warmth.

Judd swung off the horse and reached up to lift her down. His look, as their eyes met, mirrored her marvelous feeling. When her feet were on the ground, her hands remained on his shoulders as she stood close to him, unmoving.

"It's right, isn't it?" Judd murmured. "It proves that what we shared here was something special."

"Yes," Valerie agreed, a throb of profound emotion in her answer.

His mouth came down on hers to seal the wonder of their blessing. The closeness they shared was marked by a spiritual union rather than mere physical contact. The beauty of it filled Valerie with a sublime sense of joy such as she had never experienced in his arms. It was nearly as awe-inspiring as the miracle they had witnessed.

When they parted, she was incapable of speech. Judd let her turn from his arms and followed silently as she made her way across the clearing to the place where their son lay. She knelt beside him, staring for a moment at his sleeping tear-streaked face.

"Tadd, darling." Her voice sounded husky and unbelievably loving. "Wake up! Mommy's here."

He struggled awake, blinking at her with the misty eyes of a child that had suffered a bad dream and still wasn't certain it had ended. She smoothed the rumpled mop of brown hair on his forehead and wiped his damp cheek with her thumb.

"Mommy?" His voice wavered.

"I'm here," she assured him.

"I didn't mean to run away." His lips quivered. "I was going to come back after I got a puppy. But I couldn't find Judd's house, and I . . . I couldn't find you."

"It doesn't matter," Valerie said to dismiss the remnants of his fear. "We found you."

She gathered him into her arms, letting his arms wind around her neck in a strangling hold as he began to cry again. Judd crouched down beside them, his hand reaching out to hold Tadd's shoulder.

"It's all right, son," he offered in comfort. "We're here. There's nothing to be frightened about anymore."

Tadd lifted his head to stare at Judd, sniffling back his tears. Almost immediately he turned away and buried his face against

Valerie. Hurt flickered briefly in Judd's eyes at the rejection in Tadd's action.

"I think he's embarrassed to have you see him cry," Valerie whispered the explanation.

The stiffness went out of Judd's smile. "Everyone cries, Tadd, no matter how old he is," he assured the small boy, and was rewarded with a peeping look. Like Tadd, Valerie had difficulty in imagining that Judd had ever cried in his life, but his quiet words of assurance had eased the damage to a small boy's pride. "Come on," said Judd, rising to his feet, "it's almost dark. It's time we were getting you home."

Tadd's arms remained firmly entwined around her neck. At Judd's questioning look, Valerie responded, "I can carry him," and lifted her clinging son as she rose.

Judd mounted the gray horse and reached down for Valerie to hand him Tadd. When Tadd was positioned astride the gray behind him, Judd slipped his foot from the left stirrup and helped Valerie into the saddle in front of him. The gray pranced beneath the extra weight.

"Hang on, Tadd," Judd instructed, and a pair of small arms obediently tightened around his waist. Judd turned the gray horse toward the farmhouse.

CHAPTER TEN

Twilight was purpling the sky as they approached the house. Judd reined the gray horse toward the paddock gate and leaned sideways to unlatch it, swinging it open and riding the horse through. Stopping in front of the porch, he reached behind him and swung Tadd to the ground, then dismounted to lift Valerie down.

"Thank the Lord, you found him!" Clara came bustling onto the porch as if she had been standing at the window watching for them.

"A little frightened, but safe and sound," said Judd, his hand resting lightly on Valerie's waist. He glanced down at her, smiling gently at the experience they had shared.

Tadd went racing onto the porch. "I was going to Judd's house to see the puppies and I got lost," he told Clara. Now that he was safely back, the episode had become an adventure to be recounted.

Clara's knees made a cracking sound as she bent to take hold of his shoulders and scold him. "You should be spanked for the way you made your mother and me worry!" But already she was pulling him into her arms to hug him tightly. Tadd squirmed in embarrassment when Clara kissed his cheek, and rubbed his hand over the spot when she straightened. "If you hadn't come back before dark, I was going to call the sheriff and have them send out a search party."

"I think we're all glad it wasn't necessary," Judd inserted, and started toward the porch with Valerie at his side.

"Isn't that the truth!" Clara agreed emphatically.

"If it hadn't been for Judd, I wouldn't have found him," Valerie stated, giving the credit for finding Tadd where it was due.

"Someone else had more to do with it than I did." Judd gave the responsibility to someone higher up.

As he took the first step onto the porch, Valerie felt his gaze slide past her to the car. The moment she had been dreading ever since the house had come into sight was there. The trunk of the car was open and all of the suitcases and boxes stuffed inside were in plain sight. Judd stiffened to a halt. As his arm dropped from her waist, Valerie continued up the porch steps, a tightness gripping her throat.

"What's going on here? Is someone leaving?" His low, slicing demand was initially met with pulsing silence.

She turned to face him. Leaving after what they had just shared was going to be a hundred times more difficult, but Valerie knew it was a decision she had to stand behind. The words of response were a long time in coming.

Finally it was Tadd who answered him. "We're going back to Cincinnati. That's why I ran away — 'cause I wanted to stay here and have a puppy and mom said I couldn't."

At the cold fury gathering in Judd's gaze, Valerie half turned her head, her eyes never leaving Judd's face. "Clara, will you take Tadd in the house? He hasn't had any supper. He's probably hungry."

"Of course," her friend agreed in a subdued voice. "Come with me, Tadd." Clara ushered him toward the door and into the house.

When the screen door closed behind them, Judd slowly mounted the steps to stand before Valerie. "Is it true what Tadd said? Are you leaving?" His voice rumbled out the questions from somewhere deep inside, like distant thunder.

She swallowed and forced out a calm answer. "Yes, it's true."

"You promised you'd stay," Judd reminded her in a savage breath.

"No, I promised there'd be no more talk about my leaving," she corrected, her jaw rigid with control.

"So you were going to leave without talking about it," he accused. "You knew I was going to call. You knew I wanted to see you tonight."

"And I wanted to be gone before you did," Valerie admitted. He grabbed her shoulders. "Don't touch me, Judd. Please don't touch me," she demanded in a voice that broke under the strain. If he held her, she knew she would give in, whether or not it was right or wrong.

He released her as abruptly as he had taken her. Turning away, he swung a fist at an upright post. The force of the blow shook the dust from the porch rafters.

"Why?" he demanded in a tortured voice and spun around to face her. "Dammit to hell, Valerie! I've got a right to know why!"

For a choked moment she couldn't answer him. A welling of tears had turned his eyes into iridescent pools of anguish. She wanted to reach up and touch the sparkling drops to see if they were real or merely crocodile tears. The sight of them held her spellbound.

"When I discovered your mother knew about us . . . and Tadd, I realized I couldn't stay no matter how much I wanted to," she explained hesitantly. "Maybe if I hadn't learned that she knew, or maybe if I'd never met her, it would have been easier to stay. Now, it's impossible."

"Why is my mother to blame for your leaving?" Confusion and anger burned in his look as he searched her expression, trying to follow her logic.

"I don't really blame her." Valerie was having difficulty finding the right words. "I'm sure it's only natural that she wants to become acquainted with your son."

"You'd better explain to me what you're talking about, because you aren't making any sense," Judd warned. "In one breath you say you want to stay and in the next you're saying you can't because of my mother. Either you want to stay or you don't!"

"I can't," she stated. Her chin quivered with the pain her words were causing her. "Don't you see, Judd? What will Tadd think when he learns about us? Eventually he will. We can't keep it from him forever. I can't become your mistress. I can't put my wants above Tadd's needs."

"Then you do love me?" His hands recaptured her arms. "Valerie, I have to know," he demanded roughly.

"Yes, I love you," she choked out the admission, and averted her gaze. "But it doesn't change anything. Nothing at all, Judd." Relief trembled through her when he let her go. She closed her eyes and fought the attraction that made her want to go back into his arms.

"I wanted to see you tonight to give you this." A snapping sound opened her eyes. Judd was holding a small box. In a bed of green velvet was an engagement ring, set with an emerald flanked by diamonds. Valerie gasped at the sight of it. "And to ask you to marry me."

Her gaze flew to his as she took a step backward. "Don't joke about this," she pleaded.

"It isn't a joke," Judd assured her. "As a matter of fact, I bought the ring the day after you told me about Tadd. But I didn't give it to you before now because I didn't want you marrying me because of him."

"I don't understand," she murmured, afraid that Judd didn't mean what he was implying.

"I didn't want you marrying me in order to have a father for your child — our child," he corrected. "I didn't want you marrying me for the Prescott name or wealth. I wanted your reason to be that you loved me and wanted me as much as I love and want you."

A piercing joy flashed through her. She stared into the warm green fires of his eyes that seemed to echo the words he had just spoken. She was afraid to say anything in case she was dreaming.

"Until today I wasn't certain how much you really cared about me," Judd continued. "But when I saw the terror in your eyes at the thought that I might have been hurt by the stallions, I knew what you felt for me was real. My name and position meant nothing to you, not even the fact that I'm the father of your son."

Without waiting for an acceptance of his proposal, Judd took her left hand and slipped the ring on her finger. Valerie watched, slightly dazed, as he lifted her hand to his mouth and kissed the emerald stone that was the same vivid color as his eyes.

"You can't really want to marry me." She heard herself say. "I'm not good enough for you."

Anger flashed in his eyes. "Don't ever say that again!"

Valerie glowed under the violent dismissal of her statement, but she persisted,

"Your mother told me you'd always said you wanted your wife to have classy breeding, spirit and staying power. My background is very common."

Judd's mouth thinned impatiently, but he responded to her argument. "Class has nothing to do with a person's social position. I became acquainted with your grandfather and know you come from fine stock. That untamed streak in you proves your spirit. And as for staying power, after seven years I believe that has answered itself."

"Judd . . ." she began.

"No more discussion," he interrupted. "You're going to marry me and that's the end of it."

"Yes!" She breathed the answer against his lips an instant before he claimed hers.

An involuntary moan escaped her throat at the completeness of her love. His kiss was thorough, his masterful technique without fault. Beneath her hands she could feel the thudding of his heart, racing as madly as her own. Yet her appetite seemed insatiable.

"I thought I loved you seven years ago, Judd," she murmured as he trailed kisses down to her neck, "but it's nothing compared to what I feel for you now."

"I was such a fool then, darling," he muttered against her skin. "A blind, arrogant fool."

"It doesn't matter that you didn't love me then," she told him softly. "It's enough that you love me now."

"I was obsessed with you seven years ago," Judd confessed, lifting his head to let his fingers stroke her cheek and trace the outline of her lips.

"I was just someone you made love to." Valerie denied his attempt to have her believe she had been special to him. The past was behind them. The way he felt toward her at this moment was all that counted.

"For every time I made love to you, there were a hundred times that I wanted to," Judd replied. "It irritated me that a fiery little kitten could sink her claws into me that way. All you had to do seven years ago was crook your little finger at me and I came running. Do you have any idea how deflating it was to my masculine pride to realize that I had no control where you were concerned?"

"No, I didn't know." She looked at him in surprise.

His green eyes were dark and smoldering. There was no mistake that he meant every word he was saying. His caressing thumb parted her lips and probed at the white barrier of her teeth. Unconsciously Valerie nibbled at its end, the tip of her tongue tasting the saltiness of his skin.

"God, you're beautiful, Valerie." He said it as reverently as a prayer and moved to let his mouth take the place of his thumb, which he let slide to her chin.

He fired her soul with his burning need for her. Valerie arched closer to him, pliantly molding herself to his hard length. His hands were crushing and caressing, fanning the flames that were threatening to burn out of control. Just in time, he pulled back, shuddering against her with the force of his emotion and rubbing his forehead against hers. He breathed in deeply to regain his sanity.

"Do you see what I mean?" he asked after several seconds. The rawness in his teasing voice vibrated in the air. "I never intended to make love to you that first time, but your kisses were like a drug that I'd become addicted to. After a while, they weren't enough. I needed something more potent. Even if you hadn't been willing, I would have taken you that first time. It isn't something I'm very proud to admit."

"But I did want you to make love to me, Judd," Valerie assured him, hearing the disturbed shakiness in her own voice. "Foolishly, I thought it was the only way to hold you. Also, I wasn't satisfied anymore, either. I wanted to be yours completely and I thought that was the way."

"If you hadn't, there are times when I think I might have crawled all the way to your grandfather to beg his permission to marry you. That's how completely you had me under your spell," Judd told her, and rubbed his mouth against her temple. "But it's something we'll never know for sure."

"No," Valerie agreed. "And I wouldn't want to turn back the clock to find out. Not now."

He couldn't seem to stop slowly trailing kisses over her face. His gentle adoration was almost worshipful, while Valerie felt like a supplicant begging for his caresses. This freedom to touch each other with no more self-imposed restraints was a heady elixir to both of them.

"When I made love to you that first time and realized no other man had ever touched you, I was filled with such a self-contempt and loathing that I swore I'd never come near you again," Judd murmured. "I felt like the lowest animal on earth. Then you confronted me with your justifiable accusations that I'd abused you for my pleasure and dropped you, and I was lost."

"I thought you were avoiding me because I was so inexperienced," Valerie remembered, her fingertips reaching up to explore his jaw and curl into his hair. "Because I hadn't satisfied you."

"It was never that," Judd denied. "You were a wonder to me. I wanted you to know the same feeling of fulfillment that you gave me."

"Judd, there's something I want to ask." Valerie hesitated, hating to ask the question, yet after his revelation it troubled her.

"Ask away," he insisted, lightly kissing her cheekbone.

Her hands slid down to his chest, her fingers spreading over the hard, pulsing flesh. Eluding his caressing mouth, she lifted her head to see his face, and the contentment mixed with desire that she saw reflected in his eyes almost made her dismiss the question as unimportant and as trivial as all that had gone before them.

"Why didn't you ever take me anywhere, ask me out on a date?" she finally asked the question, her look soft and curious.

Judd winced slightly, then smiled. "You were my private treasure," he explained. "I wanted to keep you all to myself. I wanted to be the only one who knew about you. I guess I was afraid if I took you somewhere someone might steal you from me. So I kept trying to hide you, but I ended up losing you anyway."

"Only for a time," she reminded him and sighed. "I thought it was because I was just Elias Wentworth's granddaughter, not worthy enough to be seen in the company of a Prescott."

"I know. Or at least, I realized it that last time we met," he qualified his statement. "I was angered by that. But I was more worried that someone at the party you were so anxious to attend might take you from me. And I suddenly questioned whether you hadn't been meeting me just to eventually obtain an invitation to one of the Prescotts' parties in order to meet someone else. I was enraged at the thought that you might be using me."

"Judd, you didn't!" Valerie protested incredulously, frowning.

"Jealousy is an ugly thing, darling," he admitted, "especially the obsessively possessive kind. Mine was almost a terminal case."

"You don't need to be jealous. Not now and not then," she told him, her throat aching from the love she felt. "There's never been anyone else but you. Oh, I've dated a few times these last seven years," she admitted in an offhand manner that said those dates had meant nothing. "But it seemed that if I couldn't have you, I didn't want to settle for second best."

Judd kissed her hard, as if grateful for the reassurance and angry that he had needed it. "The week after we argued and you stormed away, I practically haunted our place. Then I went into town and overheard someone mention that you'd gone away. For a while I told myself I was glad you'd left because I could finally be in control of my own life again. When I found myself missing you, I tried to make believe it was because you'd been such a satisfactory lover."

"And it wasn't that?" she whispered hopefully. Her hands felt the lifting of his chest as Judd took a deep breath before shaking his dark head.

"No, it wasn't that," he agreed. "After six months, I finally accepted the fact that mere lust wouldn't last that long. That's when I rode over to your grandfather's to find out where you were. Remember that filly I told you I bought from him?"

"Yes," Valerie remembered.

"That's the excuse I used." There was a rueful twist of his mouth. "It took me a week of visits to get the subject around to you.

When he finally did mention you, it was to tell me you'd eloped with some man."

"But —"

"I know." Judd staved off her words. "It wasn't true, but at the time I didn't know it. I almost went out of my mind. Half the time I was calling myself every name in the book for letting you go. Or else I was congratulating myself on being rid of a woman who could forget me in six months. But mostly I was insane with jealousy for the man who now had you for himself."

"And I was trying so desperately to hate you all that time." Her voice cracked and she bit at her lip to hold back a sob. "Seven years." So much time had been wasted, unnecessarily.

"Everybody pays for his mistakes, Valerie," he reminded her. "What we did was wrong and we both had to pay. My price was seven years of visiting your grandfather and listening to him talk about your happy family and his grandchild and all the places your husband was taking you to see. I had seven years of endless torture picturing you in another man's arms. While you had to bear my child alone and face the world alone with him."

"In Tadd, I had a part of you. I loved him even more because of that." Valerie hugged him tightly to share the pain they had both known.

"When your grandfather died and Mickey told me you were coming for the funeral, I vowed I wouldn't come near you. I didn't think I could stand seeing you with your husband and child. But I couldn't stay away from the house."

His voice was partially muffled by the thickness of her tawny hair as his mouth moved over it, his chin rubbing her head in an absent caress. "I think I was trying to rid myself of your ghost. I was almost hoping that having a child had ruined your figure and being married would have turned you into a nagging shrew — anything to rid me of your haunting image. Instead you'd matured into a stunningly beautiful woman who made the woman-child I loved seem pale in comparison."

"When you walked out of that door, I nearly ran into your arms," Valerie admitted. "It was as if those seven years we were apart had never existed."

"If I hadn't believed you had a husband somewhere, that's exactly what would have happened," he said, and she felt his mouth curve into a smile against her hair. "It wasn't until that night that I found out you didn't have a husband. It was as if the heavens had just opened up and I tried to rush your surrender."

"Before I came back, I thought I'd got over you. All it took was seeing you again to realize I hadn't," she confessed. "I fought it because I knew how much you'd hurt me the last time and I didn't think I could stand it if that happened again. And I . . . I thought all you wanted was to have me back as your lover."

"My lover, my wife, my friend, my everything," Judd corrected fiercely. "It was after the funeral that I told my mother about our affair seven years ago and that this time I was going to marry you no matter how I had to make you agree. But first I had to try to convince you to stay."

"I thought you were trying to set me up as your mistress when you offered to lease the farm," Valerie remembered.

"I was," he admitted. "I knew you still felt a spark of desire for me."

"A spark?" she laughed. "It was a forest fire!"

"I didn't know that," Judd reminded her. "I was simply desperate to try anything that would reestablish what we once had. Later I could persuade you to marry me."

"But when you found out about Tadd . . ." Valerie began.

"Yes, I had the weapon," he nodded. "I knew that for his sake I could persuade you to marry me. That's when I realized that if you married me without loving me, the hell of the last seven years would be nothing compared to what the future would hold. I had to find out first whether you felt more than sexual attraction for me."

"Have I convinced you?" She gazed into his face, her eyes brimming with boundless love.

His mouth dented at the corners. "I'll be convinced when you stand in front of a minister with me and say, 'I do.' And if I can arrange it, that day will come tomorrow."

"The sooner the better," Valerie agreed, and couldn't resist murmuring the title, "Mrs. Judd Prescott . . . Valerie Prescott. It sounds beautiful, but I'm not sure it's me."

"You'd better get used to it," he warned. "Because it's going to be your name for the rest of your life."

"Are you very sure that's what you want?" Just for an instant, she let herself doubt it.

"Yes." Judd kissed her hard in punishment. "As sure as I am that our next child is going to be born on the right side of the blanket."

"What about Tadd?" Valerie began.

Only to be interrupted by Clara ordering,

"Tadd! Come back here this minute!" from inside the house.

A pair of stampeding feet raced to the screen door and pushed it open as Tadd came rushing out, staring wide-eyed at the embracing pair. "Clara said we might not be leaving after all!" he declared. "Is it true, mom? Are we going to stay?"

"Yes," Valerie admitted, making no effort to move out of Judd's arms, not that he would have permitted it.

"Till summer's over?" he questioned further.

"No, you're going to live here," Judd answered him this time.

Clara came hustling to the door, scolding, "Tadd, I thought I told you not to come out here until I said you could." Her shrewd blue eyes glanced apologetically at Valerie. "He bolted out of the kitchen before I could stop him."

"It's all right," Valerie assured her, smiling into the twinkling eyes.

"Does that mean I can have a puppy?" Tadd breathed in excited anticipation.

"You not only can have a puppy, you're also going to have a father," Judd told him. "I'm going to marry your mother. Is that all right with you?"

"Sure." Tadd gave his permission and

switched the subject back to a matter of more urgent interest. "When can I have my puppy?"

"In another couple of weeks," Judd promised. "As soon as it's old enough to leave its mother."

"That long?" Tadd grimaced in disappointment.

"It's better than seven years," Judd murmured to Valerie as his arm curved more tightly around her waist.

"It will go by fast, Tadd," Valerie told him. "In the meantime, you can choose the one you want and play with it so it will get to know you."

"Can I go over now? I know which one I want," he said eagerly.

A wicked light began to dance in Judd's green eyes. "Clara might be persuaded to take you," he suggested. "While you're playing with the puppies, she could be helping my mother make arrangements for the wedding reception tomorrow."

"And leave you here alone with Valerie?" Clara scoffed at the very idea of it. "As virile as you are, Judd Prescott, there'd be a baby born eight months and twenty-nine days after the wedding!"

Judd chuckled and Valerie felt her cheeks grow warm at the thought. He glanced down at her, his gaze soft and loving.

"She's right," he said. "After seven years, I can wait one more night. Because it's the last night we're ever going to be apart. I promise you that, Valerie." Unmindful of the small boy and the older woman looking on, his dark head bent to meet the toffee gold of Valerie's.

We hope you have enjoyed this Large Print book. Other Thorndike Press or Chivers Press Large Print books are available at your library or directly from the publishers.

For more information about current and upcoming titles, please call or write, without obligation, to:

Thorndike Press
P.O. Box 159
Thorndike, Maine 04986 USA
Tel. (800) 223-1244 or (800) 223-6121

OR

Chivers Press Limited
Windsor Bridge Road
Bath BA2 3AX
England
Tel. (0225) 335336

All our Large Print titles are designed for easy reading, and all our books are made to last.